She needed to get away.

But no sooner had she stood when her daughters left her side and went straight to the man she wanted to avoid.

When she caught up to them, the girls were chatting away with Noah and his mother.

"Millie, Margaret, don't be pests," Shauntelle said.

"She invited us over," Millie told Shauntelle, as she pointed at Noah's mother. "Can we go ride the horses?"

"I don't think so." She gave her daughter a gentle tug, but Millie pulled away, throwing Shauntelle off balance. As she began to fall, a strong arm snaked around her waist.

Noah held her closer than she liked, creating a curious mix of discomfort and assurance. "Are you okay?"

"I— Yes. Thank you." She looked up at him, ready to pull away. But then their eyes met and in their depths she saw an indefinable emotion. Regret? Sorrow?

She found herself unable to look anywhere but at him. Her heart rolled over in her chest as the warmth of his arm registered. Even as one thought echoed in her brain.

This man is responsible for your brother's death.

Carolyne Aarsen and her husband, Richard, live on a small ranch in northern Alberta, where they have raised four children and numerous foster children and are still raising cattle. Carolyne crafts her stories in an office with a large west-facing window, through which she can watch the changing seasons while struggling to make her words obey. Visit her website at carolyneaarsen.com.

Books by Carolyne Aarsen

Love Inspired

Cowboys of Cedar Ridge

Courting the Cowboy
Second-Chance Cowboy
The Cowboy's Family Christmas
A Cowboy for the Twins

Big Sky Cowboys

Wrangling the Cowboy's Heart
Trusting the Cowboy
The Cowboy's Christmas Baby

Lone Star Cowboy League

A Family for the Soldier

Refuge Ranch

Her Cowboy Hero
Reunited with the Cowboy
The Cowboy's Homecoming

Visit the Author Profile page at Harlequin.com for more titles.

A Cowboy
for the Twins

Carolyne Aarsen

Recycling programs for this product may not exist in your area.

 LOVE INSPIRED BOOKS

ISBN-13: 978-1-335-50929-1

A Cowboy for the Twins

Copyright © 2018 by Carolyne Aarsen

www.Harlequin.com

Printed in U.S.A.

And God shall wipe away all tears from their eyes;
and there shall be no more death, neither sorrow,
nor crying, neither shall there be any more pain:
for the former things are passed away.
—*Revelation* 21:4

For my beloved father,
whose life was a reflection of his faith.

Chapter One

That did not sound good.

Shauntelle's hands tightened on the steering wheel of her car as the engine's whining grew louder. She eased off the gas and the ominous racket quieted, but as soon as she accelerated, it got worse.

Definitely not good.

"What's that noise?" Millie called out from the back seat of the car.

"I think it's the sound of trouble," Shauntelle muttered.

And that's when smoke streamed out from under the hood.

Shauntelle braked, pulling over as far as she dared to the side of the road as the cloud grew. The scent of coolant leaking assaulted her nose.

"What's going on?" Millie released her seat belt and hung over the front seat of Shauntelle's subcompact vehicle.

"Why did you stop?" Margaret echoed her sister's concern, but she stayed obediently buckled up as she looked up from the book she'd been reading.

"My car is not cooperating with my well-laid plans," was all she said, turning the engine off at once.

Shauntelle hid her frustration from her seven-year-old daughters. According to her budget, this little car needed to last her at least another year. She had bigger priorities.

After her husband Roger's death in a car bombing in Afghanistan two years ago, Shauntelle had grieved, railed against life and, to her shame, Roger. He was doing a temporary job, working for Doctors Without Borders, a dream of his since he had graduated med school.

He had died on one of those trips.

Shauntelle couldn't afford to stay in Vancouver and because she couldn't rent, let alone buy, a place of her own, she moved in with her parents in Cedar Ridge, Alberta. The girls settled into school, and at her brother Josiah's urging, she started making plans for a restaurant in Cedar Ridge. It had been a lifelong dream of hers, and things were finally coming together.

However, the dream did not include a car breakdown. Especially not when it was full of baking deliveries she needed to finish by the end of the day.

She clutched the steering wheel as she inhaled, practicing what her grief counselor had told her. Pull back. Let go. Focus on the next thing you can do.

And commit everything to the Lord.

Since Roger's death, Shauntelle had struggled with God. When Josiah died in a construction accident only a year ago, she really felt betrayed by Him.

But she knew she had nowhere else to go, and so she slowly found her way back to God. After the major things she'd dealt with, however, she didn't think it proper to pray for a car.

She pulled in another breath, a tiny curl of panic starting in her belly.

She opened the hood, then coughed on the acrid smoke billowing out of the engine.

"What are you going to do?" Millie asked, hanging out of the back passenger window.

"Push this car off a cliff," Shauntelle muttered as she pulled up the strut that supported the car hood and stood back, her arms crossed over her chest as she fought down the panic.

"You can't do that, Mommy." Margaret sounded frightened.

"Just having an automotive temper tantrum, honey," Shauntelle assured her very sensitive daughter. "I'm not driving it anywhere. Besides, there's no cliff handy." The road they were on had only three people living on it. An older couple from Calgary only used their summer house from June to September. Carmen Fisher, the manager of Walsh's Hardware and the T Bar C, was another resident, and then there was the Cosgrove Ranch.

Carmen was working today, so she wasn't home. And it was the end of April, which meant no one would be at the other house either.

That left the Cosgrove Ranch, a couple of miles down the road.

Not an option.

"Call Grandpa," Margaret suggested, getting out of the car and walking around to the front to join her mother.

"Grandpa and Gramma are working." And she was not putting any extra pressure on them.

She didn't have any cousins or relatives she felt comfortable calling out to the back of the beyond. Nor did she have AMA, so phoning a tow truck meant she had to pay for it herself. And what would that cost?

"Guess we'll have to walk to the highway," she said. Some of the deliveries consisted of meat pies, and though they were in a cooler with ice, she didn't know how long they would stay fresh.

"Will we have to hitchhike?" Millie asked.

"At least it's not hot today," Margaret, ever the practical one, said. "So we won't get too thirsty."

Her daughter was right. A soft breeze swirled past them, tossing up stray leaves and pushing away the stinky smoke still drifting from the engine. A few geese honked overhead, the first harbingers of spring. Shauntelle shivered, pulling her sweater closer around her as she weighed her options. The highway was a few miles back, and neither she nor the girls had adequate footwear. They were all so excited for spring that they had put on flip-flops.

"I hear someone coming!" Margaret called out, shading her eyes against the midafternoon sun.

Hope rose in Shauntelle's heart as she heard the muted rumble of a vehicle. Maybe it was Carmen Fisher.

"They might stop," Margaret said.

"I sure hope so," Shauntelle said.

The sound of the vehicle grew louder, and then a large, jacked-up, cherry-red pickup truck crested the hill and came swooping down toward them.

Obviously not Carmen Fisher.

"I hope the driver sees us," Millie muttered, stepping closer to her mother's car.

Shauntelle hoped so too.

And then, thankfully, the truck slowed, geared down and coasted to a halt right behind her car. Shauntelle eased out a sigh of relief, but behind that came a niggle of unease. This didn't look like the kind of vehicle an elderly couple would drive.

Then she saw the driver, and her unease morphed into fury.

Noah Cosgrove stepped out of that ridiculously fancy truck, the sun glinting off his collar-length dark hair, his eyes narrowed, a leather jacket hanging on his broad shoulders and dark jeans hugging narrow hips. He looked dangerous and threatening.

Shauntelle took a step back, shielding herself with the hood of the car, her growing rage boiling up in her soul. Noah was the last person she wanted to see.

Because of Noah Cosgrove, her brother had died.

"Hey there. What's happened to your car?" Noah grinned at the twin girls who stood beside the obviously broken-down vehicle. They were thin, gangly and utterly adorable with their high ponytails, matching pink T-shirts and black leggings.

"It's smoking," one said, her eyes wide. "And Mom is trying to fix it."

"I don't think she knows how," the other said in a matter-of-fact voice. "Do you think you can?"

"Maybe." As he looked at the girls, a memory rose to the surface. Twins in Cedar Ridge were not common.

And then his heart thudded in his chest.

Of all the people to run into on the road to his mother's place, why did it have to be Shauntelle Dexter, Josiah Rodriguez's sister?

He gave himself a moment to fight the too-familiar guilt, straightened his shoulders and walked around the car. Shauntelle stood by the hood, arms clasped tightly over her chest, head held high, her brown hair drifting over her shoulders. Her flush-stained cheeks were sprinkled with freckles, and her blue eyes were narrow with anger. Clearly she knew precisely who he was.

"Hey, Shauntelle," he said, keeping his voice quiet. Nonthreatening. So far her reaction was the same as the one he had received only half an hour ago from Shauntelle's parents at the Shop Easy when he stopped there for gas and some pop. They were both working today, and while Selena Rodriguez acted reasonably civil, it wasn't hard to see Andy's fury.

"Hey, yourself," was all she said, her tone abrupt.

"So. Car trouble." He sucked in a quick breath and looked into the engine, the acrid smoke telling him everything he needed to know.

"Yes" was her clipped reply.

He gave her a cursory glance, but she was glaring at the engine ticking loudly in the ensuing silence.

"So what happened?"

"It started making a clunking noise and then it got louder."

"Can you fix it?" one of the girls asked, poking her head around the hood.

Noah shook his head. "Not with what I've got in my toolbox. I'm guessing the engine seized up."

"That sounds bad," the other girl said with a frown.

Noah took a closer look at the girls, surprised he hadn't seen the similarity between them and their mother previously. Of course, he'd had no reference point until he realized they were Shauntelle's daughters.

"It is. But let me see for sure." He flashed them a grin, then looked more closely at the engine. That's when he saw the quarter-sized hole in the engine block. He shook his head in dismay. "Sorry. It looks like a rod went through your engine. It's toast."

"So it's done?"

The rusted-out car looked like it had many better days behind it and none ahead. "Probably," he said, wishing he could give her better news.

Shauntelle pressed her hands to her mouth, and for a moment he thought she was going to cry. Not that he blamed her. From what he knew about her, she'd had a lot to deal with.

In the past two years she'd lost her husband, moved in with her parents and then, to bring it all to a tragic trifecta, lost her brother only a year ago.

Noah shoved that memory down. Josiah Rodriguez had been working for him when he fell to his death off a scaffold. And no matter how many times Noah went over the situation, how many times he tried to remind himself he wasn't to blame, he still felt at fault. He should have trained Josiah better. He should have been at the job site that day instead of chasing that other job, trying to make a few more bucks and keep his huge crew of guys busy.

"So where were you headed?" he asked, fighting the blame and self-loathing that always accompanied thoughts of Josiah. "Can I give you a ride?"

"That would be awesome," one of the twins piped up. "We're doing deliveries."

"Of what?"

"Baking and stuff," the other one put in. "My mom makes bread and buns and all kinds of goodies for the Farmer's Market. We go every Saturday, but Mrs. Fisher is in Calgary and my mom promised her and some of her other customers that she would get their stuff to them."

"I'm sure Mr. Cosgrove has other things he needs to do," Shauntelle said, a sharp tone to her voice. It wasn't hard to see she preferred he be anywhere but here.

"But he's the only one who stopped."

"Millie." The tone grew harsher as Shauntelle shot her daughter a look of warning.

Millie glanced away, her hands fiddling with the bottom of her T-shirt as she pouted.

"I'm calling a tow truck," Shauntelle said, pulling a phone out of her pocket.

While she did that, Noah took another look at the car in the faint hope he had misdiagnosed the problem. He turned on the flashlight function of his cell phone, but it only showed him the full extent of the irreparable damage.

"Is it bad?" the one named Millie asked.

He gave her an apologetic glance and nodded. "I'm afraid so."

"My mom always said this car was a beater. I thought she meant like a mixer, but my grandpa said that it meant it wasn't reliable. My grandpa is kind of smart. Just like my dad was." Millie sighed and gave Noah a wistful look. "My dad is dead. He died in the overseas. Two years ago."

"Two and a half," her sister corrected, her mouth pursed as she clutched her book. "And it's not in the overseas, it's just overseas. It was in Afghanistan. He was a doctor without borders. We used to be sad, but now we're not so sad anymore. My name is Margaret and my sister's name is Millie."

"I'm sorry for you," Noah said. He'd heard bits and pieces about Roger Dexter from Josiah whenever Noah stopped by the work site. Josiah had been proud of Roger, and when he was killed, Josiah was devastated. Noah gave him a week off to be with his parents and sister.

Now Josiah was gone as well.

Noah wondered again about the wisdom of coming back to Cedar Ridge. But he had made a promise to his mother and his cousin Cord, whose wedding he had come to attend, and he couldn't back out now.

"My daddy was a hero," Millie put in. "That's what my grandpa says. A genuine hero."

Noah experienced a tinge of melancholy at the girl's admiring words. A doctor working selflessly for other people. That was the very definition of *hero*. "He sure was," he agreed.

"Not for two hours?" Shauntelle's annoyed cry broke into the conversation. She clutched her cell phone in one hand, the other grabbing her head. "Okay. I guess I don't have a choice."

She slid her phone in the back pocket of her blue jeans, her hands clasped around the back of her neck. It wasn't hard to read the frustration on her face.

"That's a long wait," Noah said.

"Yep." Shauntelle massaged her neck with her hands, then dropped them on her hips. "Well, girls, guess we're stuck here for a while."

An awkward silence fell at that. Noah knew he couldn't leave Shauntelle here. The road dead-ended at his mother's ranch. If Carmen Fisher was in Calgary, she wouldn't be back for a couple of hours. There was only one other family who lived down this road.

"Do you know if Mr. and Mrs. Anderson are home?" he asked.

"They only come in the summer," the other twin said with a tone of resignation. "No one else will come down this road."

And his mother couldn't help them out either. She hadn't been feeling well the past few weeks, which was one of the reasons he'd made the trip back to Cedar

Ridge. She hadn't been diagnosed with anything specific. Some vertigo, some headaches, low iron. Just worn and weary, was all she would tell him.

"Can you help us do deliveries?" Millie asked. "You have a big truck."

"Mr. Cosgrove is probably busy." Shauntelle's voice held an undertone of condemnation. "I'll try Leanne. Maybe she can help. She's got a big SUV."

She punched in another set of numbers, which was followed by a few seconds of silence. Guess that was a no-go too. He saw the battle on Shauntelle's face, and he knew she fought her anger with him and the reality of her situation.

"I don't mind helping," he said.

"Okay. Fine." She tossed out the words like they were poison. "I need to make a delivery to Mrs. Fisher's place. If you could bring me back to my parents' house after, that would be great."

"But what about all the other stuff?" Millie put in. "You said we need to deliver them to get enough money for the eggs in your nest."

Noah repressed a grin at the mash-up of the term.

"Can you help us deliver those too?" Millie asked, turning to Noah and giving him a mournful look.

He shouldn't give in. Shauntelle didn't want to go with him any more than he wanted her to.

"If we don't get them to the customers they'll be no good," the other twin said. "Some of them are perishable. Like the meat pies."

"Mr. Cosgrove probably has far more important things to do." Shauntelle spoke quietly, but there was enough of a sting in her voice to bother him. "And my nest can manage without the extra money."

"But that would be wasteful," Millie wailed.

"I'm just going to my mom's place," Noah said. "I don't have much else planned."

"Does your mom live just before Mrs. Fisher's?" Millie asked, her eyes suddenly wide. "Does she own the place with the big gate?"

"That's it. The T Bar C." His father's ranch. As a young man, he couldn't leave it fast enough. He had returned from time to time but only for a quick visit. He hadn't come back for the past year. Since Josiah Rodriguez died working for him, shame and guilt had kept him away from the ranch and Cedar Ridge.

But his cousin's wedding had brought him back. He knew he couldn't get out of that obligation. While here, he hoped to convince his mother to finally let go of the ranch. Sell it and move with him to Vancouver. After Josiah died on his job site, Noah had hung on to the business long enough to deal with the inquiries and inspections. Then he sold it. He currently had a line on a new business he wanted to start, a small trucking company. It would be a fresh start in a different business.

He knew his mother hoped he would come back to the ranch, take it over and keep the Cosgrove legacy going. That wasn't happening. To him, the ranch had always been a symbol of relentless, backbreaking work, a demanding father who was never satisfied.

Cedar Ridge didn't hold any special memories for him.

"That's such an awesome place. I love it," the little girl said excitedly.

"It is a nice place." He was surprised to hear a faint note of melancholy in his voice as he looked at his childhood home through her eyes.

"So, can you help us out by driving us around?" Millie asked. "So we can get more money in our nest?"

He glanced Shauntelle's way. He saw she wasn't keen on the idea, but at the same time he didn't feel right leaving her stranded here.

"Sure. I can help you out."

"Well, what are we waiting for?" Millie said, shooting her mother an expectant look.

Shauntelle blew out a sigh of resignation. "I guess we don't have much choice."

"Just one thing, though," Noah said. "I'd like to stop in and see my mother. Make sure she's okay before we head out."

"Of course," Shauntelle said.

"So first off, let me know what you need from the car," Noah said.

Shauntelle walked to the hatchback, yanked it open and pulled out one of the three coolers, indicating the other two with her chin. "I need all those, and there's a carrier with muffins as well."

Noah nodded and hefted one cooler out, set the second one on top and carried them both to his truck. "We can put them in the box or the back of the truck," he said.

"Box is fine."

"I'll drive slow. That way you won't have to worry about your baking getting squashed. Don't want you to have to give anyone a discount." He added a grin to show he was kidding, but she didn't smile.

While he hadn't been in the same grade as Shauntelle growing up, he knew enough about her. Knew that she had a keen sense of humor and was quick with a comeback.

But the weary-looking woman in front of him bore

no resemblance to that fun, spunky girl. And he felt that he had contributed to the faint lines bracketing her cheeks and marring her forehead.

He set the coolers on the ground by the rear of the truck, popped open the tailgate and slid them all in. He hopped on board in one easy motion and pushed them to the front of the box. He shifted his heavy toolbox to keep two of them from sliding around, though he was sure they'd be okay.

Then he jumped down.

"You're really good at that," the other twin said, her voice full of admiration.

"Doesn't take much skill," he returned with a half smile. "But I'm used to climbing ladders and jumping off roofs."

Millie frowned in confusion. "What do you do?"

"I'm a contractor. Carpenter," he corrected.

Millie nodded, her frown deepening. "Our uncle Josiah was a carpenter too. But he died when he fell down. My mom said his boss was a greedy man, and that's why my uncle died."

Her innocent voice spelling out the reasons for Josiah's death hit him like a sledgehammer to the chest.

"I'm sorry about your uncle," was all he said.

At that moment, he happened to glance at Shauntelle. The sorrow on her face was replaced by a tightening of her lips, a narrowing of her eyes.

He shouldn't be surprised. During all the inquiries and investigations and follow-up by the various boards and organizations, he had occasionally run into Shauntelle's parents and got a clear idea what they thought of him.

But Shauntelle's reaction bothered him more.

He spun around and headed to the car to close the

hatch just as Shauntelle walked in the same direction. They almost collided, and instinctively he reached out to steady her.

For a split second, she stayed still, getting her balance before jerking her arm away. She ducked inside the car, coming out with two booster seats.

"Do you want me to put those in the truck?" he asked.

Shaking her head, she walked back to his truck to do the job herself. A few minutes later the girls were buckled in, the car was locked up—even though Noah doubted anyone would steal it—and they were headed down the road to Mrs. Fisher's.

The drive to Carmen's place was quiet. What do you say when a young girl inadvertently accused you of being greedy and the cause of her uncle's death? Trouble was, he felt it was true in spite of what the reports had said.

Might-have-beens crowded into his mind, creating their own regret and pain.

He eased out a breath, trying to ignore the woman on the seat beside him. Shauntelle sat as close to the door as physically possible, as if giving herself maximum distance between them.

"This is a really nice truck," Millie said from the back seat of the crew cab. "Lots of room."

"I like the color," the other twin said.

"Red is Margaret's favorite color," Millie put in authoritatively. "She wants to paint her room red when we get our own house. But Mom said we can't until the restaurant is finished and it starts making money. I want to paint my room pink."

"That sounds nice," Noah said, going along with the

conversation. Anything to break the awkward silence between him and Shauntelle.

"So are you Mrs. Cosgrove's son?" Millie asked.

"Yes I am."

"Are you Noah Cosgrove?"

"Guilty as charged," he returned, then realized how that sounded. Too on the nose, he thought.

Another beat of silence followed his comment.

"Our uncle Josiah worked for you." This came out sounding like an accusation.

"Yes. He did." Noah shot a quick glance in the rear-view mirror at Millie, who sat behind her mother.

She frowned, as if absorbing this information. Then she looked over at Noah. "You don't look like an evil man."

"Millie, that's enough," Shauntelle said quietly.

"But he doesn't. He looks like a nice man and he's helping us."

Shauntelle turned to the girls, and Noah caught a warning glance sent her daughter's way. Millie got the hint and looked out the window.

They pulled up to Carmen's place and Noah got out, the girls' innocent words hounding him. "What do you need?" he asked.

"I'll get it myself." She sounded tired, so instead of listening to her, he got out of the truck as well and climbed up into the box.

"Tell me what I should grab," he asked, opening the coolers.

"The muffins and the two loaves of bread from the box and the meat pie from the cooler. They're marked with Carmen's name."

Noah found what she described and handed them to her.

Taking them, she turned and walked away. Noah got out of the truck box and watched her as she strode up the graveled path to Carmen Fisher's house, her thick brown hair shifting and bouncing on her shoulders. She had an easy grace and presence. He remembered being vaguely aware of her in school.

And then, one summer, it was as if she had blossomed, and she had really caught his attention.

Trouble was he was dating Trista Herne, and Shauntelle was four years younger than he was. While that meant little now, in high school it was a vast gulf he couldn't breach. So he kept his distance. And then, as soon as he had the diploma in his hand, he left. The first time he had come back was for his father's funeral six years later. By that time, Shauntelle was gone.

"That's a cute house too," Millie said, hanging out the window she had opened. Clearly she didn't mind that he was "an evil man."

"It is," Noah agreed. "It's part of the T Bar C. The ranch foreman used to live there." Noah adjusted his hat, dropping his hands on his hips as his mind shifted back to times he had tried to erase from his memory. Long days and nights working until he could barely stand. Fencing, building sheds, herding cows, baling hay and stacking bales. There was always work to do.

He remembered one evening he had been baling in a field just past this house. The tractor broke down at the far end of the field. Terrified of what his father would say, he stayed with the tractor. Then Doug and Julie had come home early from their outing. They brought him supper, and while he ate, Doug repaired the tractor. Then he sent Noah home and finished the baling himself. His father, however, was furious that he had made Doug work on his day off.

"Why doesn't the foreman live there now?"

"My mother doesn't need a ranch foreman," he said as he got back into the truck.

"Why not?"

"The ranch doesn't have as many cows as it used to." He wished his mother would sell them. She had to hire someone to feed the cows and the horses that she wouldn't sell either.

Noah suspected it was a way of recognizing the hard work his father had done to make up for the way Noah's grandfather ran the T Bar C into the ground with his poor management. Though his father had struggled to bring it back to its former glory, low commodity prices had made it almost impossible. He worked like a dog and made sure Noah did as well. He'd died from a heart attack when he was feeding the cows. Noah often felt that the hard work, stress and his father's personality had combined to cause his death.

Shauntelle came back and got into the truck, giving him a tight nod. "Thanks."

"So you're okay with stopping to see my mom?" Noah asked.

"I can hardly complain," Shauntelle said with a note of asperity.

He sensed it was difficult for her to spend time with him, but she had no choice.

They drove just half a kilometer back down the road and under the imposing gate of the T Bar C.

"That's an awesome gate," Millie said, craning her head to get a better look.

"It should be," Noah said. "I helped build it."

"Really?"

"Yep. Took me and my dad two days and a lot of stress to get it up."

He stopped as he heard the bitter note that entered his voice. Too well, he remembered being perched on the top of the upright, reaching for the cross beam his father was raising with the tractor. The near miss as the beam swayed and almost knocked him off. The anger his father spewed at him even though it wasn't his fault.

No, the T Bar C held no memories he wanted to nurture.

They drove down the winding drive lined with elm trees his great-grandmother had planted in a fit of optimism. To everyone's surprise, they flourished and now created a canopy of shifting shadows that teased the sunshine filtering through.

"Wow. This is beautiful," the girls breathed.

Then they turned a corner, and the log ranch house came into view.

It was perched on a hill with a small creek flowing in front of it. A wooden bridge arched over it. Flower beds, in various states of neglect, stair-stepped up the side of the hill toward the imposing log house.

"That's the coolest house ever," Margaret breathed, unbuckling and leaning over the seat.

"Did you build it?" Millie asked.

"No. My grandfather did. He was a carpenter as well as a rancher." Noah shot a sidelong glance at Shauntelle to gauge her reaction. Though she had lived here most of her life, she had never been on the ranch, to his knowledge.

Her eyes were wide and her mouth formed an O of surprise. Then, as quickly as that came, her features shuttered and her lips pressed together.

He guessed she was comparing his place with her parents', a place he had seen from time to time.

And though his parents' financial circumstances had nothing to do with him, he couldn't get rid of a sense of shame.

And, even worse, guilt.

Chapter Two

"Who all lives in that fancy house now?" Margaret asked, hanging over the front seat of Noah's truck.

"Just my mom," Noah said.

"That's a big house for one person," Millie said. "She must rattle around in it. That's what my mom always says when she sees big houses."

Shauntelle wanted to reprimand Millie, but it would only draw more attention to her comment. Right about now Shauntelle was having a hard enough time stifling her own reaction to Noah's place and his presence. She struggled with a mixture of frustrated fury with him and an older, traitorous attraction.

Noah Cosgrove had always been one to make young girls' hearts beat faster. At one time, so had hers.

But he was older. Then he'd left, and her life moved on.

Now here she was, a widow responsible for two children and full of plans for a future of her own. Roger had been a good man, but it seemed they spent most of their married life chasing after his dreams and plans, to the detriment of their family life and finances.

She learned the hard way that it was up to her to

make something of her life. She couldn't count on anyone else's help. Now she was determined to make a future for herself and her daughters by way of her restaurant. This would require all her energy and concentration.

Besides, after what happened to Josiah, Noah was so far off her radar he may as well be in another solar system.

Noah pulled the truck up in front of a double garage. "Home sweet home," he said, but Shauntelle heard a puzzling tone in his voice. Sarcastic almost.

"I'll just be a minute," he said, walking to the door.

Millie was about to get out to follow him when Shauntelle caught her by the arm. "Stay here. Mr. Cosgrove just wants to say hello to his mother, and we should let them do that alone."

"But I want to see the house," her daughter cried.

"Doesn't matter. Stay put."

"I want to see it too," Margaret added.

"Learn to live with disappointment," Shauntelle said in a wry tone, though she was talking as much to herself as she was to her daughter.

Part of her would have loved to see the inside of this very impressive home. She was always interested in floor plans and the layout of rooms. Someday she hoped to build her own house, though it would never approach the size of this place.

She looked over the massive expanse of lawn that needed mowing spread out in front of the house, the flower beds that had seen better days and the older hip roof barn beside them. Beyond that were rail fences and pastures all flowing toward the mountains guarding the valley where the house was situated.

It was a showpiece, that was for sure. However, no

swing sets stood in the yard, no play center or sand-box. No sign that, at one time, a young boy had lived here. She knew Noah had been an only child, but still.

Her parents' yard still had the old tractor tire sand-box she and Josiah had played in, as well as the rickety swing set the girls liked to play on.

But nothing here.

A few moments later the door of the house opened, and to Shauntelle's surprise, Noah and Mrs. Cosgrove came out.

She looked tired and frail. Her once-dark hair hung in a gray bob. The gray-and-pink-striped tunic she wore over leggings seemed to hang on her narrow frame. Shauntelle had seen Mrs. Cosgrove in town from time to time and at church once in a while. Though she couldn't be more than sixty, she looked far older.

"I told my son I wanted to say hello to you," Mrs. Cosgrove said, waving at them as they came nearer. "He said he was helping you make deliveries."

"My mom's car broke down," Millie announced, clambering out of the truck before Shauntelle could stop her. And where Millie went, Margaret followed.

They gathered around Mrs. Cosgrove, looking all demure and sweet. It would be rude if she stayed in the truck, so Shauntelle came to join them as well.

Mrs. Cosgrove gave her a gentle smile, holding her hand out to her. "And how are you doing, my dear? You have been through a lot. First your husband and then your brother."

Shauntelle was surprised Mrs. Cosgrove mentioned Josiah in front of Noah. But she swallowed an unwel-come knot of sorrow and gave her a faint smile.

"It's been difficult," she said. "But I have my girls

and the community, and I've gotten a lot of support from my parents as well."

"They are good people and I'm so sorry for their loss, and yours as well when your brother died." Mrs. Cosgrove took her hand in both of hers, looking into her eyes.

Her sympathy was almost Shauntelle's undoing, but she kept it together. She did not want to cry in front of Noah and his mother.

"My gramma said that Uncle Josiah worked for an evil man," Millie put in, shattering the mood and moment. "That's why he died. But Mr. Cosgrove doesn't look that evil."

Shauntelle felt like grabbing her dear daughter and covering her mouth, but it was too late.

Again she saw pain and anger flit over Noah's face. Again she wondered how much he took to heart.

Mrs. Cosgrove looked from Millie to Noah, her own features twisted as she withdrew her hand.

"Sometimes we only know part of the story," she said. "But I won't keep you long. I understand you have lots of deliveries to do. I wanted to say hello. I hope to see you tomorrow at the Farmer's Market. You will have a table there, won't you?" she asked Shauntelle.

"Yes. I will. If you have anything specific you want me to make, you are more than welcome to put in an order."

"That's fine, my dear. Maybe I'll let Noah pick something out. He's especially fond of chocolate cake."

"I'm fond of *your* chocolate cake," Noah corrected.

His mother gave him a gentle tick with her fingers. "You never say that in front of another woman," she said.

"Sorry. Forgot about the female code." Noah's smile

held a touch of melancholy, and Shauntelle thought it must be difficult for him to see his mother like this. "But you better get back to your easy chair, and we better get going." Noah motioned with his head to the house.

Mrs. Cosgrove glanced over at Shauntelle. "He makes me sound like I've got one foot in the grave. Which is quite a physical feat, considering the graveyard is about ten miles away."

Shauntelle chuckled at that, but she could see from the puzzlement on Millie's and Margaret's faces that she would be in for several questions from them about that phrase.

"You run on now and take care of those meat pies," Mrs. Cosgrove said, holding her cheek up to Noah for a kiss. "I'll see you later."

And before Noah could protest, she turned and walked back to the house.

Noah watched her go, and Shauntelle could see that he was torn.

"We don't have to do this," she said. "You can bring me straight to my parents' place, and then come back sooner."

He turned to her with a wry smile. "She'd never let me come back until I was done helping you, so we may as well carry on."

His smile made him look more approachable. And his attitude around his mother generated a rift in her own feelings toward him.

But she shook that off. She couldn't afford to let herself get soft around him.

She had her children to think of, her business to plan and her parents to comfort and support.

Besides, she heard he was only in Cedar Ridge for

his cousin's wedding, and then he would be gone again. Which worked out well. She didn't think she could be around him any longer than that.

"I can't believe you let that man take you on your deliveries." Selena Rodriguez's pinched and lined lips and narrowed eyes made a far more eloquent statement than her clipped sentence.

"I didn't have much choice, Mom," Shauntelle said as she loaded the dishwasher. "The ice in the coolers holding the meat pies was already half-melted. By the time the tow truck came, I wouldn't have felt right about delivering them. And that would have been a waste, and I would have had unhappy customers." Besides, she'd sensed Noah would not have let it go.

It had made for an extremely uncomfortable situation. Trying to keep her anger at him under control while appreciating what he was doing for her.

She was trying as hard as she could to develop a good reputation, both for her food and her delivery service. She wanted customers to know she was dependable and trustworthy. She hoped building up all this goodwill would keep her in good stead when it came time to open her restaurant.

"You could have called us," Selena muttered, rinsing out a rag and wiping down the counters.

"I tried, but there was no answer. Dad must have been out pumping gas, and you were probably busy somewhere else. Besides, I didn't like the idea of making you take time out of your workday to come and rescue me."

"I would have come for sure if I'd known Noah Cosgrove picking you up was the alternative." Her mother's voice broke, and Shauntelle once again struggled with her own variable emotions.

The name Noah Cosgrove always engendered an unhealthy indignation in the Rodriguez household. Noah had been Josiah's boss, and her brother died while working for him. Josiah had often complained that Noah pushed everyone too hard.

After Josiah's death, there had been inquiries and phone calls and meetings, and it was as if they relived his death again and again.

Noah was exonerated, but Shauntelle still struggled with forgiveness and anger. Had he not worked her brother so hard, Josiah might still be alive.

"Well, they're done."

As for her girls, all was right in their world in spite of the emotions swirling around their heads.

Supper was over and her father sat in the living room reading one of his favorite Thornton Burgess books to the girls. Though she doubted they were that terribly interested in the adventures of Reddy Fox, they were too polite to say any different. And it kept them busy while her mother fussed.

"I'm thankful Dad could take care of the car," Shauntelle said. He had arranged for a friend to pick it up and bring it to the wrecker. "I should have brought it in to the mechanic when I had the chance. Dad's been warning me for months to get it fixed."

Though part of the problem was she hadn't had time to bring it to the mechanic. Between juggling her part-time job at the bank, baking and gardening for the Farmer's Market and her work to get the restaurant going, extra time was hard to find. And next week she would be even busier working with the contractor who was finishing the arena.

The restaurant she wanted added had never been in the original plans. She had her own blueprints drawn up at great expense, which meant she would have to work closely in the next few weeks with the contractor to make sure everything meshed.

"You could have bought a new car with that money you got from when Roger passed away."

"You know I need that money for my restaurant and eventually my own place." She gave her mother a teasing grin as she put the containers holding leftovers in the refrigerator. "I'm sure you don't want me and the girls staying here forever. Kind of cramps Dad's and your style."

"You know we enjoy having you around," her mother said with a gentle smile. "If you'd had a new car you wouldn't have had to get a ride with…Noah Cosgrove," her mother added.

The evil man.

Millie's words still made Shauntelle squirm. She would have to make a note to discuss with her mother how she talked about Noah. The girls didn't need to get pulled into the drama and emotions surrounding her brother's death.

"It was okay, Mother," she said, trying to keep her tone light. She knew she would run into Noah sooner or later, so maybe it was just as well she got it over and done with.

Though she was still surprised at how difficult it had been to be around him. She couldn't keep the image of her brother's coffin out of her mind. The searing pain of lowering her brother down into the ground. The loss of her own dreams and plans.

She and Josiah had talked of starting the restaurant together, and he had promised once he was done working for Noah, he would come on board. Now that dream was gone too.

"I can't believe he's back. Acting as if nothing has happened." Her mother's voice broke as she folded her arms over her stomach, leaning back against the kitchen counter. Shauntelle felt the usual sympathy blended with her own grief. "He came around the store today to get gas, if you can imagine."

"Maybe it was the closest place," Shauntelle suggested, trying to rise above her own reactions. Sometimes she was tired of how much they had ruled her life recently.

Her mother harrumphed. "He could have gone to the Petro Pumps. It's just down the road."

"Or he could've just been trying to give you some business."

Her mother frowned at her. "And why are you defending him? Josiah was your brother. If it wasn't for Noah, he'd be still alive."

Shauntelle knew this was her cue to stoke the fires of her mother's anger, and normally it wasn't difficult to do. But today she was bone weary and simply didn't have the energy.

"I know," was all she said.

"Are you okay, honey?" her mother asked, her voice still thick with emotion. "Are you thinking of Josiah too?"

"I sometimes wonder what he would be doing right now." She easily slipped into one of her mother's favorite conversations—imagining a life for Josiah had he not died.

"Probably working for your father. Maybe taking over the gas station."

Shauntelle doubted that. One of the reasons Josiah

had originally talked about working with her on a restaurant was to avoid exactly that scenario.

"He'd probably be traveling," she said. "Where do you think he would go?"

Her mother said nothing for a moment, then looked back at her, her eyes dull. "Doesn't matter, does it? He's gone. And Noah is here. I don't know how I'm going to handle that."

The sorrow in her voice was Shauntelle's undoing, and she hurried over to her mother's side and pulled her into her arms. "You can pray about it, Mother. You've always said you receive your strength from the Lord."

Her mother sniffed, nodded, and then pulled back. "Yes. If it wasn't for my faith, I don't know how I would have gotten through this dark time." She tugged a tissue out of the box close at hand and dabbed at her eyes. "But I just hope Noah is only here for a short while. I'm not ready to face him for too long."

Shauntelle knew she wasn't either. Seeing Noah had been a shock on so many levels. He'd always been the boogey man. The "evil" man. The man who could create a twist in her stomach at the sheer mention of his name.

But even before that, he'd been someone who intrigued her. Someone she, at one time, had spun futile dreams around.

She shook the emotions off. He wasn't for her, and she didn't have room for him. She was being utterly foolish giving him even one second of her thoughts.

Chapter Three

"Think you'll sleep okay tonight?" Noah bent over his mother and brushed a kiss across her forehead.

She sat up in her bed, propped against a ridiculous number of pillows with an equally ridiculous number of books stacked on her bedside table and the floor beside it. A small diffuser steamed beside her bed, filling the room with the rich aroma of one of the many oils she had lined up in front of it.

"Of course I will," she said with a smile, setting aside her book. "Thanks again for dinner. It was very good."

"Takeout from the Brand and Grill," he said with a grin as he perched on the edge of her bed. "Dining at its finest."

"I enjoyed it. I enjoy anything I don't have to make myself."

Noah glanced around the room, unable to quash the feeling that he was invading his mother's privacy. His parents' bedroom was the one room in the house that was off-limits to him, and he was only allowed in by invitation.

"Too bad I came back so late. We could have gone out for a walk after supper," he said.

"That's okay. I'm looking forward to our trip to the Farmer's Market." She gave him a sly smile. "Maybe Shauntelle made some chocolate cake after you said it was your favorite."

"I highly doubt Shauntelle cares one way or the other that I like chocolate cake."

His mother's expression grew serious. "I know that family doesn't think highly of you, but I'm sure Shauntelle knows better."

Noah thought of the "evil man" comment Millie had made, and the anger simmering in Shauntelle's eyes. "I'm not so sure. Besides, it doesn't matter what she thinks."

"I'm glad you could help her get all her deliveries done though."

He should have known that his mother wasn't going to leave the subject of Shauntelle alone. To his surprise, they hadn't talked about her at suppertime. Instead, his mother had brought him up-to-date on all the comings and goings of the Walsh clan. Cord's wedding and Morgan's future one, and now his other cousin, Nathan, was engaged as well. All this was delivered with a careful sigh directed to Noah.

He easily read the subtext. When would he get married?

"I'm glad I could too," he said, keeping his tone casual. "And the entire time I got a running commentary from Millie about all the people we brought the baking to."

His mother chuckled. "Those girls are quite the pair. For twins, they sure are different though. Millie is such a pistol, and Margaret is so quiet." Then she grew serious, her dark eyes suddenly intent. "And how was Shauntelle with you?"

Noah held her gaze for a few beats, then sighed and looked away, knowing what she was referring to. "Uptight. Tense. Angry. I think she would have preferred not to accept my help, but she was stuck."

His mother covered his hand with hers, squeezing lightly. "Don't take it personal, son. She's had a lot to deal with recently. It has to be hard being a widow and taking care of her children. Roger Dexter was a good man, and I'm sure she misses him."

He noticed that she deliberately left Josiah out of the conversation. As if she wasn't sure where to put the death of Shauntelle's brother either.

"Roger died in Afghanistan, didn't he?" Noah continued, sticking with an easier topic.

His mother nodded. "He often worked overseas. In fact, he was working with Doctors Without Borders when he was killed. He wasn't military, but in my mind he was a real hero."

"Sounds like it," Noah said, though even as he spoke the words a small part of him wondered why anyone would want to leave a wife and twin girls behind. If he had a family, he would never stay far away from them. He'd keep them close.

If.

The closest he had come to settling down was with Holly, his former fiancée. But somehow, after he proposed, things changed. She became more demanding of him and his time. Which made him wonder what would have happened on the job site that day if he hadn't given in to her constant pleas to be doing something, going somewhere. Would that have stopped Josiah from going up on that man lift? Would he have maybe given him yet another safety lesson just to make sure?

"You look pensive," his mother said, poking him gently.

"I do that to put people off," he said, once again pushing his memories down. "My dark hair and glowering eyes keep people away."

"You shouldn't do that, you know." She spoke quietly, smiling, but Noah heard the faint warning in her voice. "Keep people away. I know that Josiah's death has affected you more than you admit, but you weren't found to be at fault."

Maybe not, but that didn't stop him from feeling guilty that he hadn't been there. He caught her concerned look again and forced a smile. "I know. But that doesn't change what happened to him. Or how his family feels."

Shauntelle's strong reaction to him earlier still stung.

"They just need time." She patted his arm. "So how long are you sticking around?"

He held her yearning gaze, feeling the weight of all the years he had stayed away dropping on his shoulders. "I had figured on staying until Cord's wedding. Then I'm off to Vancouver to see about a new business." He hadn't made a final commitment yet, but his mother didn't need to know that.

She gave him another one of her pensive looks. "I wish I could think of something that could make you consider staying. Permanently."

Another picture of Shauntelle flashed into his thoughts. She had always been attractive, but she was older now, and even though life had dealt her some harsh blows she was, if possible, even more beautiful than she had been when he left Cedar Ridge.

As quickly as the memory came, he dismissed it.

Shauntelle, with her hero husband and banked anger, was out of reach.

"You know Cedar Ridge doesn't hold a lot of good memories for me," he said. "Neither past nor present. I have no intention of sticking around here longer than I have to."

Too late, he realized how harsh that sounded. He tempered his comments with a smile. "We'll have fun together, and once you move to Vancouver, then we'll spend a whole lot more time together," he said. "It's a beautiful city, and the winters are much milder than our Alberta winters."

"We'll see." She gave him a sorrowful smile, and he could tell he hadn't convinced her to leave yet. "I know you want me to sell the place. It's too hard to run with hired help." She waited a moment, holding his gaze with hers. "I guess I had always hoped you would come back," she continued, sounding wistful. "And maybe now that you're here…"

"Please don't," he said, interrupting her hopeful words. "Cedar Ridge hasn't been my home for a while, and certainly can't be now."

"Does your father still have such a strong hold over you?"

His mother's mournful voice created a mixture of feelings. Resentment that she should ask when she knew precisely what he had gone through, blended with emotions he had struggled against for most of his life. Where had she been while his father was being so hard on him? Why hadn't she stood up for him? Taken his side?

"You haven't forgiven him, have you?" she continued.

Noah pulled in a deep breath and shrugged his shoulders, trying to settle the sorrow he knew he should have been done with long ago.

"He's not around to forgive, so it doesn't really matter anymore does it? Besides, it's memories too." He gave his mother an apologetic smile.

"I pray for you every day," she said. "That you can find it in your heart to forgive your father. I think when you do, you will find your way back to your other Father. The one who loves you perfectly. His love will give you real peace."

"You don't have to worry about my faith life," he said finally, pushing down the wavering emotions his mother's words created. For the past few years he and God had had an understanding. Noah wouldn't bother God, and God wouldn't bother him.

Besides, God wouldn't want to have much to do with someone who couldn't even take care of his own employee.

Someone who would never, ever be referred to as a hero.

Like Shauntelle's husband was.

"Mom, can I put those out?" Millie pointed to the cooler holding the layer cakes Shauntelle had spent hours baking last night and icing this morning. Her mother had let her use her car until she figured out what to do about transportation, but it was tiny and Shauntelle had worried about how the cakes would travel in the little hatchback.

"I'll take care of them, honey," Shauntelle said, hurrying over. There was no way she was letting anything happen to those cakes after all the work she'd put into them.

She had found the cakes while she was on Pinterest

and plunged down the rabbit hole that is the internet. When she read the recipes, she was intrigued. If people liked them, they could be potential dessert menu items for her restaurant.

"How long do we have to stay here?" Margaret asked, shivering as she pulled her jacket closer around her. "And why couldn't we be inside today?"

"Just a few weeks ago you were wishing we could be outside." Shauntelle tapped her daughter playfully on her nose.

Though she found the weather a bit cool herself, she was still glad to be outdoors. Last week they had set up in the multipurpose room of the old arena, stuck in a damp, echoing space that was always too noisy and cramped.

The new arena couldn't be completed soon enough, for the other members of the Farmer's Market or her. Next week she could finally implement all the ideas roiling around in her head ever since she'd come up with her plan for a restaurant and snack bar.

For a moment she felt a shiver of panic. What if all her plans for her own business were a waste of time and money? What if she was fooling herself, thinking people would want to come to her restaurant for dinner? Cedar Ridge already had the Brand and Grill in town, plus Angelo's, and she heard the bakery had just set up a bistro.

Was there room for her restaurant? Would she make enough to take care of herself and her daughters?

She struggled to fight down the anxiety she always felt when doubts about her decision attacked her. And lately they'd been coming harder the closer she came to implementing them.

But she wasn't a quitter. She'd put her husband

through med school, raised the girls on her bank salary while Roger pursued his dream and vision during his internship. She put in long hours to make sure they had the basics in life. And after Roger died, she dug back into her emotional reserve and carried on. She fought her own sorrow and put on a brave face for her daughters while her own heart was breaking. And now she was supporting her parents through their own grief over the loss of their son and her brother.

As well as dealing with her own grief and anger.

She hadn't quit then, and she wasn't about to quit now. Through it all she had depended on her Lord to give her the strength she needed, and He hadn't failed her yet. Come what may, she knew she always had her faith.

"That looks really nice, Mommy," Margaret said, full of admiration as Shauntelle set out the third fancy layer cake.

"I thought they turned out well," she said, with a touch of pride, as she shifted the one chocolate cake with its fancy trimming to show it off the best. While she did, she imagined cakes, cheesecakes, pies and fancy squares lined up on shelves in a glass case at the entrance of her new restaurant, tempting the patrons even before they sat down to order dinner.

She'd set up far too many boards on Pinterest with ideas for decor, layout, furniture and menus. It was endless, and she often had to stop and prioritize.

"Sweetheart, can you set out the muffins?" she asked Millie as she set some loaves of bread on the shelf in front and to one side of her table.

"I want to see what Rory has," she grumbled. "She told me she would have some new jewelry when she came this week."

"I want to see too," Margaret chimed in, abandoning her job.

"Later. The market will be open in ten minutes and I want to be ready."

"Hey, girls!" Sonya called out, dragging two rolling suitcases past Shauntelle's table. Sonya DeBree was short and heavyset, her dyed black hair worn in a perpetual braid down her back. The young woman stopped and whistled loudly. "Wow, those cakes turned out fantastic. I'd ask you to save one for me, but I think I've got enough cake stored up in me to last me until I die." She massaged her protruding belly, laughing as she did so. "Once you start that restaurant I'm going to be in such trouble."

"I hope so," Shauntelle said with a wry look.

Sonya must have caught the hint of concern in her voice. "It will be just fine. Here's hoping those construction people can get the arena done in time though. Heard things were slowing down." Then, before Shauntelle could ask her what exactly she meant by those unsettling comments, she swished her long skirts and headed off to her table to set up her spices, homemade jam and condiments on her table.

Shauntelle felt a tremor of unease at her comment, but then shrugged it off as Farmer's Market gossip. The usual chitchat of people who had time on their hands and a listening ear.

She turned her attention to getting the last of her baking set out. Ten minutes later everything was ready, and people were already drifting into the parking lot where they were set up, wandering around the tables.

A few people came directly to her table. These were her regulars who showed up every Saturday to pick up preorders that she couldn't deliver.

"Thanks so much, Mrs. Michaels," Shauntelle said as she handed the elderly woman the tray of muffins and cookies she had just bought. "Are you sure I can't tempt you with a hazelnut torte cake?"

The tiny, bird-like woman just laughed, showing her crooked teeth as she hooked the bag over her walker. "Sugarplum, if I bought that I would eat it all myself and end up fatter than I already am."

Considering she couldn't weigh more than ninety pounds, even with her walker, Shauntelle thought that highly unlikely.

"I might be tempted to buy one."

Shauntelle looked over at her newest customer, and there was Mrs. Cosgrove. Then her heart plunged when she saw Noah join her.

His dark hair and equally dark eyebrows arching over hidden, deep-set brown eyes could have given him a menacing look, but she remembered that melancholy smile of his yesterday. In spite of how bitter she was over what happened to Josiah because of him, seeing Noah face-to-face made it difficult to know exactly what to do with her anger.

"I thought my son should find out firsthand how good the baking that he delivered yesterday actually is," Mrs. Cosgrove said.

Shauntelle dragged her attention away from Noah, granting Mrs. Cosgrove a more genuine smile. Fay Cosgrove was a loving, caring woman who, when Shauntelle had come here, had gone out of her way to support and encourage her. It wasn't hard to separate her feelings for Noah from this woman.

"I'm glad you came. I hope you can find something."

"I'm sure I can." Mrs. Cosgrove's smile grew but

then she seemed to wince and shook her head. "Sorry. Feeling a bit punk yet."

"Should we go home?" Noah asked.

"I'm fine. Just a bit tired." Mrs. Cosgrove waved off his concern. "I'm tempted to get one of those cakes, though Noah will have to step up and do his part to finish it."

"I don't think that will be much of a hardship." He turned to Shauntelle again. "Do you have any meat pies today? I know when we were delivering them, they looked and smelled pretty tasty."

"I have a few," she said, disappointed at the flush his compliment gave her. It felt wrong.

"My mommy just made these cakes." Millie walked over to where Noah was standing, and to Shauntelle's embarrassment, grabbed his hand, dragging him closer to the table and directly in front of Shauntelle. "She said they were an experiment, but I think they look awesome."

"More of a trial run," Shauntelle hastened to explain, far too aware of his towering presence. "For the restaurant. Thought I could offer them as desserts."

"They look really nice, Millie," he said, addressing her daughter instead of her. For some reason that bothered her.

"I helped my mom bake them," Millie said, folding her hands in front of her and rocking back and forth, obviously pleased with Noah's attention.

Yeah, he had that effect on women and girls of all ages, Shauntelle thought, remembering how she, too, had once admired him from afar.

"You didn't help that much," Margaret put in, coming to join them, clearly not too happy with the compliment Millie had received. "I did more."

"No you did not," Millie grumbled. "You were busy reading your book. I helped Mom mix the dough and set the timer—"

"But I mixed the icing and helped her put the cakes together."

And why did they have to pick a fight right here and now in front of the Cosgroves? In spite of their bickering, people walking past them slowed and smiled at the girls.

Every time she took the twins out, people seemed drawn to them. Though Shauntelle let them choose their own clothes and encouraged them to develop their own style, they always picked matching outfits and accessories.

Today they wore green-and-yellow-striped sweaters and hot pink leggings. If only one of them wore this outfit, they would stand out.

But the two of them, bickering and picking at each other, their ponytails bobbing, drew unwelcome attention this time.

"I don't think we need to talk about who did what," Shauntelle said with a forced smile, coming around the table and laying a warning hand on each of their shoulders. "You both helped."

"And you both did an amazing job," Noah said, crouching down to get to their level.

Which put him below hers. She could see the top of his head, the thick wave of his hair. She caught herself, frustrated at her reaction to him. She was as bad as her daughters.

"And you girls both did a great job yesterday too," Noah said, piling compliment on compliment.

Immediately the girls quit their squabbling, both looking rather smug at Noah's praise.

"So now you have to help me pick out a cake for my mother," he continued.

As Noah stood, his gaze drifted up and snagged hers. His smile slowly faded, and the serious and somber look that replaced it sent a shiver down her spine. What was he thinking when he looked at her?

Pulling her gaze away, she fiddled with the arrangement of the cakes, straightened a package of cinnamon rolls. Anything to avoid looking at Noah again. When she saw him yesterday, her anger had simmered hard, but today, after she had spent the afternoon with him, she found it had dissipated.

Until she saw her parents. Then it had returned full force.

"What do you think, Noah? Should we buy one of those?" Fay was asking.

"I think we should, but then we need to get going," Noah said to his mother. "You're still not feeling well."

The concern in his voice and the tender way he laid his hand on his mother's shoulder created battling emotions inside Shauntelle.

In spite of that, she couldn't forget the texts her brother sent her.

Texts complaining about how hard he had to work. What a slave driver Noah was. Money-hungry and pushy. Even given her brother's tendency to exaggerate, Noah still came across in those texts as a hard-nosed businessman concerned only with the bottom line.

Then her brother had died, and once again the bottom fell out of her world. She swallowed down an unwelcome knot of pain.

"You're probably right," his mother said, then turned to Shauntelle. "I think we'll take this chocolate one."

"Good choice," Shauntelle said, reaching for a box to put the cake in.

"And the meat pies," Noah prompted.

"Right. Sorry. I forgot about them." She boxed up the cake, disappointed to see her hands trembling as she closed the flaps. She wanted to show him that she was capable and in charge, unaffected by his presence, but the pounding of her heart made that impossible.

Seriously, she really had to get a handle on her emotions.

She tied a ribbon around the box and handed it to him with a forced smile. "That will be fifteen dollars."

"And the meat pies?" he reminded her.

She did a mental facepalm. "Of course." She boxed up a couple of pies and handed them to him as well, giving him the final total.

"That's pretty cheap," he said, taking them from her. "You might want to consider raising your prices."

"I'm still trying things out."

"For what?"

"The restaurant I want to start up."

"Really? That's ambitious. Where will it be?"

"It's going to be part of the arena. I'll be running a snack bar as one part of the operation with a restaurant attached to it. The contractor said he might put in a courtyard where I could have outdoor seating. People like to look at trees and flowers when they're eating, I guess, and I'm not going to argue with that. I think it will look nice." She stopped her babbling. He was making her uneasy, and she was doing that talking-too-much thing that she did when she was agitated.

He took the boxes from her, his own lips curving slightly. "Sounds like you have a good plan in place."

"I work in a bank. The only way I'd get the money

was if I had everything figured out down to how many teaspoons of baking powder I'll need."

He chuckled at that, and the shift in his expression was a surprise to her. He looked more approachable. More like the old Noah she remembered from school.

But right behind that came the memory of her brother.

"Enjoy the cake," she said, looking away.

He didn't leave, which made Shauntelle more uncomfortable.

"I know I should have said it earlier but I didn't get a chance." He took a breath, and she steeled herself for what he was going to say. "I'm sorry about your brother."

The apology sounded heartfelt and it should have made Shauntelle feel better, but if anything, it brought back her anger.

Josiah was gone, and Noah was still alive. Her parents had lost a son and she a brother. A hole in their family that could never be filled.

She didn't know what to say, so all she did was nod to acknowledge his apology. Then, as if sensing her pain and anger, Noah took a step back, turning to his mother.

"We should go, Mom. Time to get you home."

"Did you get the meat pies?" Mrs. Cosgrove asked, looking from Noah to Shauntelle. "I thought we were getting some meat pies."

"We did," Noah muttered.

But just before they could leave, someone was calling out his name and Owen Herne joined them by Shauntelle's table.

"Hey, Noah, good to see you again," Owen said, clapping him on the shoulder. "How long you back for?"

"Just for Cord's wedding, then back to Vancouver."

"So a couple weeks?"

"Probably less." He looked like he was trying to edge away, but Owen stood in front of him, blocking his way.

"Okay. I need to talk to Shauntelle and was hoping I could catch you too somewhere along the way." Owen glanced over at Shauntelle, and the foreboding look on his face wasn't encouraging. "Do you have time?" he asked Shauntelle.

"You want to talk to me here?"

He jerked his chin in the direction of the now-empty coffee table. "We could go over there."

"Give me a minute?" she asked, wiping suddenly damp hands down the side of her pants. She shot a look over to Millie and Margaret, wondering if they should be here. "Girls, why don't you go check out Rory's booth? See if she has any new jewelry."

"But I thought you said we had to stay and help," Millie said, looking very interested in whatever Owen might say.

"We need to talk, and I'd like you to go," she said.

Margaret looked like she was about to protest as well when Mrs. Cosgrove, sensing what Shauntelle wanted, walked over to the girls, taking their hands. "You know, I haven't been to the Farmer's Market in a while. Maybe you could show me around. Would that be okay?" she asked Shauntelle.

"Sure." Everyone knew everyone here, and the layout wasn't that large. Shauntelle could keep an eye on them.

"I'll come with you," Noah said.

"Actually, I wouldn't mind if you stuck around too," Owen said.

Noah frowned but nodded at his mother. "Go ahead. I'll catch up. But be careful."

"I'm not made of glass," she said with a warning

shake of her head. "Shall we go, girls?" she asked, and walked away.

Shauntelle watched a moment, but the girls seemed very comfortable with Noah's mother, chattering as they walked alongside her, pointing out the various tables.

Owen led the way to the empty table, glancing around as he did, but no one was within earshot.

When they got there, Shauntelle turned back to Owen, her heart slowly increasing its tempo. "So what were you going to say?"

"The contractor bailed on us," Owen said, dropping his hands on his hips. "Took his crew and left us in the lurch. It seems to be a recurring theme with this place. Anyhow, I thought I would tell you because you have a stake in the arena. I wanted to let you know in time so maybe you can make other plans."

"But he was supposed to help me plan out my restaurant," Shauntelle cried out. "We're installing the doors in a week or so, getting the walls put up. He had plans for my benches. My furnishings. The decor."

"Well he's gone, which means that work on the arena has officially come to an end."

And wasn't that just typical, Shauntelle thought, fighting down a wave of anger and bitterness.

One more man she couldn't count on.

Noah glanced over at Shauntelle as Owen delivered this piece of news.

Her face had gone white, and she looked like she was going to fall over. Instinctively he reached out to catch her by the arm and steady her.

To his surprise, she didn't protest his holding her up. All her attention was on Owen, and he found he wasn't ready to let her go yet. He loosened his grip slightly, but kept his hand on her arm, supporting her.

"So what does this mean for us? What are we supposed to do? Will everything get put on hold?" She stopped there, pressing her free hand to her chest, glancing worriedly from Owen to Noah as if seeking answers from them.

He wanted to put his arm around her to console her, but he was fairly sure she wouldn't appreciate it.

Owen rubbed his chin with the knuckles of one hand as he blew out his breath in a sigh. "Sorry for dropping this on you, but I just found out and I thought you should know. Seeing as how you have a pretty big stake in getting this arena done on time."

"I was supposed to open in a month and a half," she murmured. Then, as if she finally realized it, she glanced at Noah's hand still holding her arm and she pulled away.

Not that he blamed her, Noah thought. He knew what she thought of him. Each time she had seen him, her expression held a mixture of contempt and anger, which always made him want to explain, to tell her his side of the story.

Trouble was, he wouldn't be able to do a very convincing job of it. In spite of what had been reported, he still felt a wrench of guilt each time he thought of Josiah's death.

"So now we need to find a new contractor," Owen was saying. "The insurance policy we've got in place and the building permit require that the person overseeing the project have the proper qualifications."

"What about you?" Noah asked Owen. "You've been working as a carpenter for a while."

"I have, but I don't have my Journeyman's ticket, or enough experience to satisfy all the requirements."

Owen's intense gaze made Noah uncomfortable, and Noah guessed there was an underlying implication. But he wasn't biting. His plans weren't set in stone yet, but he wasn't changing anything.

"There's got to be someone around here who has his ticket or runs a company," he said, trying to keep his tone conversational.

"This time of the year, they're all booked up already. That's why we went with this guy."

"It's like this arena is never meant to be finished," Shauntelle said, wrapping her arms around her midsection. "What am I going to do about my restaurant?"

Noah felt a glimmer of sympathy for her. She'd had so many disappointments in her life already. Now this.

Don't volunteer. Don't volunteer.

Noah had to remind himself over and over not to try to fix this problem. He knew what Shauntelle and her family thought of him. There was no way he was putting himself through that every day.

"Couldn't you consider it?" Owen asked finally, going exactly where Noah suspected he had been headed from the moment he joined them.

Noah looked over at Shauntelle in time to see the look of dismay flit over her face. She met his gaze and quickly looked away.

He knew why she felt the way she did, yet it still stung. It also underlined any idea he might entertain of staying longer.

"No. I'm only here long enough for the wedding. As soon as that's done I'm gone."

"This guy leaving has left a lot of people on the

hook," Owen continued. "Just like the time Rennie left us all hanging."

"Well, that isn't my problem either." Too late, he realized how harsh that sounded.

"Could you at least think about it?" Owen asked.

"Doubt that will make much difference." He made a show of looking at his watch. "I should go find my mother. She needs her rest."

"She's coming back now," Owen said, pointing his chin toward Mrs. Cosgrove and the girls, who were chattering at her as they worked their way back through the people toward Shauntelle and Noah.

Owen said goodbye and, skirting the people wandering slowly past the tables, strode away, a man on a mission.

Millie pulled away from Mrs. Cosgrove and came running toward them, waving an intricately beaded necklace. "Look what I got."

"Millie, you didn't ask, did you?" Shauntelle said, sounding horrified.

"No. Neither did Margaret," Millie protested.

"I'm sure my mother bought it for them without them saying a peep," Noah said, glancing over at Shauntelle. "She loves buying stuff for kids. Fulfilling a need for grandchildren, I guess."

To his surprise, Shauntelle's mouth curved in a gentle smile. "She's mentioned that before. A wish for grandchildren."

"Well, that's not happening anytime soon," Noah said, then regretted the comment. Too personal.

"No girls on the horizon?" she asked, surprising him with her interest.

"Nope. Too busy with my work."

"You're not working now, though? And you're a general contractor?"

He guessed she was hinting at Owen's offer, and for some reason it annoyed him. She had made no secret of her dislike for him, but now she seemed to be asking him to help.

Trouble was, just for a moment, he'd been tempted. But he would be facing memories of pain, old and new.

"I am, but I'm only here to visit my mom and attend my cousin's wedding." Then he held her gaze, calling her out. "I don't like to be where I'm not wanted."

Her cheeks flushed but she held his gaze, as if challenging him. She looked like she was about to say something, but then someone called out.

"She's falling! Someone catch her!"

Millie cried out. Margaret screamed.

And Noah looked back in time to see his mother crumple to the ground. But what seared his soul was her hard cry of pain.

Chapter Four

Shauntelle ran over to Mrs. Cosgrove's side, just as Noah did.

"What's happening? What's wrong?" the twins called out, clinging to the older woman.

"Please leave Mrs. Cosgrove alone," Shauntelle ordered her daughters, pulling out her phone to dial 911 as Noah knelt beside his mother.

"We have a woman down at the arena grounds," she said when the emergency responders answered. "I think she broke her leg."

"Maybe just a sprain," Mrs. Cosgrove said, trying to sit up.

"Make sure she stays down," Shauntelle said to Noah, who nodded, shifting so that his mother's head rested on his lap. He tenderly pushed her hair away from her face.

And still Mrs. Cosgrove clung to her hand.

"It's okay, Mom. Just rest," he said, speaking quietly.

"My leg," Mrs. Cosgrove called out, moaning. "It hurts so much."

"Can you breathe okay?" Noah asked.

"It's hard." Mrs. Cosgrove pulled in a slow, laborious breath. "My leg hurts."

Shauntelle looked down and could see her knee lying at a decidedly awkward angle. It looked incredibly painful, but she fought the urge to straighten it, knowing that she might do more harm than good.

"Don't talk," Noah said as Shauntelle spoke to the dispatcher. Shauntelle heard the tension in his voice.

People were gathering around, and Shauntelle forced herself to concentrate and remain calm. She squeezed Mrs. Cosgrove's hand back, glancing at Noah, whose attention was on his mother.

People gathered around and Owen had returned, urging people to stand back. Advice was being tossed around, offers for help.

Millie and Margaret were still crying quietly, and in her peripheral vision Shauntelle saw Sonya take them by the hand, drawing them away and calming them down. Not that she blamed her daughters for being upset. The sight of Mrs. Cosgrove's leg was enough to make even a seasoned EMS worker blanch. She wished she dared do something more, but she didn't even have pain medication on her.

Her chest tightened, and she clung to Mrs. Cosgrove's hand. Then Fay Cosgrove's eyes began rolling upward in her head, and Shauntelle hoped and prayed nothing more serious was going on. The sound of wailing sirens grew closer and Shauntelle prayed harder.

Dear Lord, please keep this woman safe. I can't let my children see this.

She knew her prayer sounded selfish. She should be praying for Noah, but she was a mother too, and right now her main concern was for her daughters. They'd had so much loss and sorrow in their lives.

Noah's hand covered hers. She knew he was just trying to connect to his mother, but the feel of his rough palm, the hands of a workingman covering hers produced a surprising ache inside her.

A tremble of loneliness.

She wanted to pull her hand away. This was Noah, after all, but she stayed where she was, not wanting to cause Mrs. Cosgrove any further distress.

Finally, the ambulance pulled up, and the crowd parted as the EMS team rushed toward them.

Shauntelle slowly extricated her hand from Noah's and his mother's and got up to give the paramedics room, but Noah wouldn't leave.

The ambulance crew snapped out a few questions as they got Mrs. Cosgrove stabilized. Noah answered them as Millie and Margaret ran to join her, clinging to her hand.

"Is she going to die?" Millie wailed.

Shauntelle caught Noah's panicked glance and she shushed her daughter, shaking her head.

"No. She's not," Shauntelle said, crouching down and pulling her daughter close. "Hush now. You don't want to make Mrs. Cosgrove upset."

Margaret, her less dramatic daughter, simply drifted over to Shauntelle's side, slipping her arm over her shoulder.

"I think we should pray for her," she said.

Shauntelle pulled her close, nodding. "I think so too."

One member of the EMS team pulled Noah away, asking him questions about what happened as the rest stabilized Mrs. Cosgrove's leg and gently shifted her to a stretcher.

In minutes, they were wheeling it over the bumpy

fairgrounds, Noah striding alongside, his attention on his mother and the distress clearly showing on his face.

"I hope she doesn't die," Millie sniffed, her voice catching.

"She won't die," Shauntelle assured her, holding her close. "She only broke her leg. That's all."

But Shauntelle knew that with someone as frail as Mrs. Cosgrove, there was no "only" to a broken leg. It was probably more serious than that.

"She'll be off her feet for a couple of days, given her high blood pressure," the doctor was saying, his hands in the pocket of his lab coat, his faint smile taking in both Noah and his mother, who lay on the hospital bed, her freshly casted leg stretched out in front of her. "I would prefer to keep her here overnight—"

"No, I want to go home," his mother said, with a firm shake of her head. "I'm not that sick."

"No, but you haven't been feeling well," Noah said, wishing his mother would take the doctor's advice. He wasn't sure he liked the idea of being responsible for his mother's care.

"If you do want to leave, then we'll have to arrange for a home care nurse to stop by twice a day for the first week and then every other day until your cast is off."

"Which will be when?" Noah asked.

"About six to eight weeks."

"That's almost two months," his mother cried out. "How will I plant my garden?"

"Good thing Noah's around," the doctor said. "He can help you."

"That's true," his mother said, reaching out to take Noah's arm. "And he's such a big help to me."

They both seemed to assume he was sticking around.

Trouble was, he knew there was no way he could leave as soon as he had planned.

"I like to do what I can, where I can," he said, stifling a sigh.

This changed and complicated everything. It went without saying that he would cancel his holiday.

Then he'd have to contact the owner of the trucking company in Vancouver. See if he'd be willing to hold off until he got everything settled here.

"So we'll see you in a week," the doctor said to his mother, and then turned to Noah. "And I'm glad you can stay. This will make your mother very happy."

He wasn't sure if it was the guilt he perpetually felt when it came to his mother that made him feel the doctor was hinting at something more.

"A happy mother is a peaceful mother," was all he said.

The doctor made sure his mother had her prescription for painkillers, advised her about posthospital care, then handed her over to a nurse, who followed up with advice, and then helped his mother into a wheelchair.

Fifteen minutes later, her prescription was filled, the home care nurse had set up an appointment and his mother was ensconced in the back seat of his truck, her leg stretched out in front of her.

"You sure you're okay?" Noah asked, angling his rearview mirror so he could see her better.

"I'm fine," she said, and truth to tell, she did look pretty good for having broken her leg only a few hours ago. "We should let Shauntelle know how I'm doing. I'm sure those girls will be concerned. Maybe we could stop by the Farmer's Market and show them I'm okay?"

"I'm sure the market is over by now," Noah said. He wasn't too keen on facing Shauntelle again.

"No. It goes until two o'clock. It's only one now. And I forgot to get my cake."

"Mom, you just broke your leg. You're run-down and tired. You need to go straight home and to bed."

His mother frowned at that but then nodded, as if finally realizing the wisdom of what he was saying. "Okay. But you have to promise me that you'll call her as soon as we get home."

"I don't know her number." And he wasn't about to call the Rodriguez home to get it.

"I have it right here," his mother said, reaching for her purse. "I took one of her business cards."

Noah didn't know if it was the painkillers the doctor prescribed for her or the fact that he was now at her beck and call for eight weeks, but for a woman who had just broken her leg, she seemed awfully chipper.

"And you can ask her about the cake," his mother added. "Ah. Here it is." She pulled out the card and waved it at him. "Here's her number."

"I'll get it from you when we're home," was all he said.

Thankfully that seemed to satisfy her, and she sat back, humming a quiet song.

But by the time they got home, the painkillers seemed to have eased off. She wasn't humming as much. When he helped her out of the truck, she wavered and he decided to forgo the crutches they had picked up at the pharmacy. He ignored her protests, scooping her up in his arms and carrying her to the house instead.

He managed to get the door open one-handed, and when he stepped inside the house his mother sighed.

"You know, your father carried me over the threshold of this house when we were first married," she said, smiling a loopy smile. "He was such a romantic."

Noah only nodded, unable to reconcile the man he knew with the husband his mother was remembering.

"He was a good man, you know," she said, her voice taking on a faintly defensive tone.

"I'm sure he was," was all Noah would say as he brought his mother to her bedroom. There was no way they were having this discussion now. He settled her on the bed and went back for her crutches and purse. When he came back, she was staring out the window. He followed the direction of her gaze. The house was set atop a hill, and from her window she could see the barn and the paddocks connected to it. Beyond that he caught a glimpse of one of the pastures. A few cows grazed in the field, a small fraction of the herd that he and his father had taken care of. Which, he knew, was a remnant of the original herd that his mother's grandfather had, at one time, run. The ranch had fallen far from those glory days. Days his father had tried so hard to return to.

"Your father poured so much of himself into this place," his mother said, as if sensing the direction of Noah's thoughts. "He wanted so bad for me to see it back as it was when my grandfather ran it."

Noah said nothing to that. Though he loved his mother, he often wondered whether she knew how his father had treated him and turned a blind eye, or if she really didn't know.

If it were the former, reminding her of that would only make him bitter that she hadn't taken his side. If it was the latter... Did it really matter anymore? His father was gone and the ranch was fading. It was time for the ranch to be sold and this part of his life to be over.

"I'm going to see about supper," Noah said, turning back to his mother. "You just rest."

"I will, but you make sure to call Shauntelle about that cake. And those meat pies."

"Of course," he said. He would have preferred to leave it be, but he knew his mother wouldn't let go until he did as she requested.

"The card is in my purse. Just take it out of there."

Noah did as directed. "I'll call her right away."

She smiled at him, then turned her head, pulled the blankets around her and closed her eyes.

He left, closing the door quietly behind him. As he walked down the hall to the kitchen, he flicked Shauntelle's card between his thumb and forefinger, not sure what to do. Shauntelle and her daughters confused him. He preferred to keep his distance, for his own sake as much as anything else. Which meant he had to make up some excuse when his mother's cake didn't show up. Poor cell service, or Shauntelle didn't answer his call.

Once he was in the kitchen, however, a new dilemma faced him. He had to make supper, and he had no idea what was in his mother's house. He opened her refrigerator and was dismayed to see that all it contained was two eggs, half a jug of milk, a small tub of margarine and a few containers with questionable contents.

The freezer held an open box of frozen waffles, a single frozen burrito, some fish sticks and, inexplicably, a large bag of ice. And when he went downstairs to check the chest freezer, it was gone.

Eggs and waffles it was, he thought with a sigh, yet another flash of self-reproach washing over him as he trudged back up the stairs. No wonder his mother had been feeling so poorly. If this was any indication of her eating habits, he was surprised she was as spry as she was.

He'd have to get some grocery shopping done tomorrow.

He was about to pull his phone out to make a grocery list when he caught the flash of light off a vehicle pulling into the yard. Frowning, he walked around the counter and to the door just off the kitchen.

As he stepped outside, his heart did an unwelcome leap in his chest. Shauntelle was getting out of her car.

One of the twins hung out the back window and waved at him, grinning. "We're bringing you your cake and meat pies!" she shouted. Then the back door opened and the girls piled out.

"I told you to stay in the car," Shauntelle called out, closing the door with her foot, her hands full.

"Is your mom okay?" one of the girls asked, running up to him. "Will she live?"

This one was Millie, he guessed, from the way her bandanna hung crooked on her head. The other, Margaret, looked more put together. More reserved. But she was right behind her sister, looking just as eager for news.

"Millie," Shauntelle reprimanded her daughter, then gave Noah an apologetic smile as she followed the girls. "Sorry. She's a bit dramatic."

"I kind of guessed that," Noah said.

"We brought you your cake and meat pies," Margaret put in, her hands folded primly in front of her. "We told Mom that you paid for it and we had to deliver it, just like we do for all the other people who order her stuff."

"Well, thanks for that," Noah said. In spite of his discomfort around Shauntelle, he was truly grateful for the meat pies. At least he and his mother would have something more substantial than waffles and eggs for supper.

"How is your mother?" Shauntelle asked, concern edging her voice.

"She's resting. Verdict is a broken leg, but I think you probably figured that out."

Shauntelle winced as if remembering the awkward angle of his mother's leg. "How long will she have to have the cast on?"

"Six to eight weeks."

Shauntelle nodded slowly, as if absorbing this information. Then she held out the boxes she was carrying. "And here's your purchases. The top box is the cake, the other two are the meat pies." She handed over the stack of pink-and-white-striped boxes, which he recognized from helping make her deliveries.

"Thanks again." His hands brushed hers as he took them and, to his surprise and dismay, he couldn't stop the faintest tingle of awareness at the contact.

He shook it off, getting a firm grip on the boxes, not sure what to do next. It would seem rude not to invite them in, but he could see from the way Shauntelle was edging away that she was anxious to leave.

"This is a really nice house," Margaret said, grinning at him.

"Thank you."

"We should get going, girls," Shauntelle said, confirming his suspicions.

He caught a panicked look flashing between Millie and Margaret, then the one gave the other a poke.

"Um, I'm really, um, thirsty. Can I have a drink of water?" Millie said suddenly.

"No. You can wait until we're home." Shauntelle placed one hand on Margaret's shoulder.

"And I have to go to the bathroom," Margaret said, pulling away from her mother. "Really badly." She hopped from one foot to the other, her face contorted to show him her clear distress.

Noah felt momentary confusion, not sure how to proceed. He knew Shauntelle wanted to leave, and from the way the girls were looking at him so expectantly, he had a niggling suspicion they were either stalling or trying to find a way to get into the house.

Nonetheless, he couldn't refuse a young girl access to a bathroom.

"Of course. Come in," he said, holding the door open with one hand, balancing his boxes in the other.

Shauntelle shot her daughters a warning look that they didn't catch, but Noah did.

"Yay."

"Thanks."

They scooted past him into the house, Shauntelle holding back. "Sorry about that."

"It's okay," he said, though he guessed she didn't think so from the way her lips were clamped together. He guessed the girls would receive a talking-to once they were all back in the car.

But for now, they were in his house, waiting.

"Can you tell me where the bathroom is?" Margaret asked, giving another little hop just to remind him.

"Just down the hall. First door to the right," he said, nodding with his head in the direction of the washroom.

Margaret nodded, then scooted off. Millie was about to follow when Shauntelle clamped her hand on her daughter's shoulder. "You stay here, missy," she said, her tone brooking no opposition.

But Millie didn't seem fazed.

"This is such a nice house," she said, rocking back and forth on her feet. Her bandanna fell down over one eye, and she shoved it back with an impatient flick of her hand. "It looks even bigger from the inside." She looked like she would have dearly loved to wander around, but Shauntelle held her shoulder.

"Would you still like a drink?" Noah asked, opening a cupboard door and pulling out a glass.

"Oh yes. I'm parched," Millie said, eyes wide as if just remembering how thirsty she really was.

"Seriously," Shauntelle breathed, rolling her eyes.

"I'm sorry. All I have is water."

"Water is very healthy," Millie said, flashing him a bright smile as she took it from him.

"You're a real gentleman," she said, then took a dainty sip, still looking around. "Oh, look, you can see the mountains." She took a step toward the arched entrance between the kitchen and the living room, but Shauntelle stopped her again.

"Drink up, Millie. We have to get going." She gave Noah another apologetic look. "We'll be out of your hair as soon as possible."

Though Noah sensed Shauntelle's discomfort, the girls entertained him. They were cute and fun and made the house come more alive than it had been for as long as he'd lived here.

Then Margaret joined them, also looking around the house, eyes wide. "You are so lucky to live in such a fancy house." She looked over at her sister. "The bathroom has a bathtub that you could almost go swimming in!"

"Really? Can I go—"

"To the car, girls. Now." Shauntelle's firm voice showed she meant business.

Noah guessed the girls had pushed things as far as they dared, because they gave him a quick wave of their hands, and then skipped out of the kitchen. The door fell shut behind them, and Shauntelle hesitated a moment.

"You don't need to apologize again," he said, giving her a careful smile. "Your girls are pretty cute."

"They have their moments." Shauntelle shook her head but then shared his smile, and as their eyes met, he felt it again. That peculiar jolt of awareness she'd created.

He shook it off and took a physical step away from her, as if to remind himself to keep his distance.

Her smile faded at the same time, as if she was thinking the same thing.

"Thanks for indulging my daughters, and please say hello to your mother from me," she said, giving him a tight nod.

And then she was gone.

Noah stood in the kitchen alone for a moment, the echo of the girls' happy chatter seeming to linger. He felt a moment's melancholy. He wondered when was the last time this kitchen had heard the sound of cheerful voices. He had a few vague memories of playing games here with his mother while his father was out working. Sitting up one night to see the New Year in while his father slept on the couch. But not a lot of bright chatter.

He turned away from the room, glancing out the window just as Shauntelle got into the car. She was laughing as she put her girls in the back seat. They must have said something to ease away her frustration with them.

The sight dived into his lonely soul, and he couldn't look away.

But as he watched, he saw her look back at the house and her smile disappeared.

Had she seen him watching her?

He shook off the question. Didn't matter. He would

do well to keep his distance from Shauntelle and her family.

He knew exactly how they felt about him, and in spite of everything, he couldn't help but agree.

Chapter Five

"Can we go say hello to Mrs. Cosgrove?" Millie tugged on Shauntelle's arm as the church service wound to a close. "She and Noah are in the back of the church."

Shauntelle had been far too aware of both Noah and his mother since her daughters first pointed out that she was in the back, sitting with her leg up on a chair, Noah beside her.

She suspected her daughters' newfound fascination with Mrs. Cosgrove had something to do with all the drama surrounding her breaking her leg at the market, but at the same time, their interest in Noah concerned her.

Especially when they practically barged into the Cosgrove home yesterday demanding drinks and bathroom privileges. The memory could still make her squirm. Mostly because it happened in front of Noah.

He had been on her mind too much the last couple of days. Ever since he had helped her out on Friday. Then yesterday at the market when his mother collapsed, and they had shared that moment. It was just a touch, his hand covering hers for a second. With anyone else, it would have meant nothing. But in spite of her feelings about what happened to her brother, or maybe because of them, she found herself overly aware of him.

She shook her head as if to rid herself of the notion. *You've got your life planned out*, she reminded herself. *There's no room for a man*.

She'd spent too much of her previous marriage arranging her plans and life around Roger. She needed to focus on herself and her daughters for a change.

Besides, Noah was exactly the wrong person for her. Case in point, the frown her mother was giving her daughters as the last notes of the final song rang out.

"Surrender to me that which holds you fast, Let go of hate and fear, return to me at last."

The words seemed especially apt given the uncertainty of the arena and her future.

Help me Lord, she prayed. *Help me know what to do.*

But no sooner had the prayer been formulated than her daughters scooted out of the pew and away from her.

She made a futile snatch at Millie's sweater, but both girls were already in the aisle, pushing past people in their rush to get to, Shauntelle suspected, Noah and his mother.

By the time she caught up to them, the girls were sitting on either side of Mrs. Cosgrove's chair.

"Is your leg better?"

"When will you be able to walk?"

"We sure like your house."

"Can we come visit you?"

They were peppering her with questions, and Shauntelle fought down a flush of embarrassment at her daughters' forthrightness.

"Millie, Margaret, let's not pester Mrs. Cosgrove," Shauntelle said, her voice firm, then she turned to Fay

Cosgrove. "I'm sorry for my daughters' rudeness," she said. "They are overly interested in your recovery."

Fay just smiled, patting Margaret's hand. "That's fine. I suspect I gave them quite a scare." Fay looked past her to her son. "I think I gave Noah one as well."

Shauntelle slanted a quick look Noah's way, disconcerted to see him looking at her, his expression serious.

Then he turned his attention back to his mother. "Of course you gave us a scare," he said. "As for your questions," he said to the girls, "my mom will have to wear the cast for six to eight weeks. She has crutches that she uses to get around. But she'll be okay."

Shauntelle was thankful for the assurance Noah gave her daughters. She could see they were more relieved because of it.

"But you know what," Mrs. Cosgrove was saying to the girls. "I missed you visiting yesterday. Maybe you should come again so we can talk more."

"Yay. That would be fun." Millie turned to her mother, her eyes bright with expectation. "Can we come today? They have horses."

"No, I don't think so," Shauntelle said, giving her daughters a gentle tug, wondering how to shut this down without any pushback.

"But why not? We just got invited." Millie pouted and pulled away, clearly upset with Shauntelle's reply.

But Shauntelle was still holding her hand, and Millie's sudden movement threw her off balance. Right toward Mrs. Cosgrove's leg. She flailed her arms to avoid hitting her, and then a strong arm snaked around her waist, pulling her away.

Noah held her closer than she liked, creating a curious mix of discomfort and assurance.

"Sorry," he said, holding her flustered gaze as she

struggled to regain her balance. "I thought you were going to fall against my mother."

"I thought so too. Thanks for stopping me." She finally got her feet under her, looking up at him, ready to pull away.

But in the dark brown depths of his eyes she saw an indefinable emotion. Regret? Sorrow?

She found herself unable to look away as it became suddenly harder to breathe. Her heart rolled over in her chest as the warmth of his arm registered.

He is responsible for your brother's death.

Just then Owen Herne joined them, giving her a chance to reorient herself. Get herself emotionally as well as physically centered.

"How are you doing, Mrs. Cosgrove?" Owen was asking.

"Oh, I've been better," she said, flashing a weak smile. "Millie, can you hand me my crutches?" she asked, her hand on the back of the chair to hold her balance.

Millie was only too happy to oblige.

"So I heard you need a contractor for the arena," Mrs. Cosgrove was saying as she fitted the crutches under her arm.

"Yes. The guy we had hired quit on us." Owen's heavy sigh easily reflected Shauntelle's own feelings about the situation.

"Noah's a contractor, and he's got to hang around for a while." Mrs. Cosgrove turned to him. "Don't you think this will be a perfect opportunity to help out the Rodeo Group?"

Shauntelle caught Noah's narrowed eyes, and for a moment she felt sorry for him. His mother reminded her of her daughters. They liked to use public moments for their own agenda.

"Would you?" Owen asked. "I know I mentioned it before. It would be a lifesaver. We've got volunteers and some licensed guys, but we can't do the work unless we have a general contractor. Which you are."

"If you help, my mommy can get her restaurant," Margaret put in, hanging on to his arm. "She really, really wants this restaurant. I heard her say so to my gramma, even though she thinks you're an evil man."

Shauntelle felt a very unwelcome flush warm her neck and cheeks. Seriously, what had gotten into her daughters? Since meeting Noah and his mother, they had lost all semblance of decorum.

She turned to Noah to apologize yet again when she caught a wry look creep across his face.

"Sounds like this might be a chance to redeem myself," he said.

"Or help the town out," Owen put in. "You're right here. It would take us weeks to find someone else, which would put everything on hold."

Shauntelle found herself holding her breath as various emotions battled within her.

Could she work with him?

Think of your restaurant. The sooner it gets done, the sooner you can make plans for your own future.

"My mother's health is my first priority," he warned.

"I'll be fine," his mother said, waving off his concerns. "You need to help the town get this arena done, and Shauntelle needs her restaurant going."

Shauntelle wanted to protest his mother's defense of her but stopped herself. It was true.

Noah shot her another glance, as if measuring how she felt about this. She wasn't crazy about the idea. She knew her parents would be livid, but it wasn't their business on the line.

"I would need to leave from time to time to see how my mother is doing, and if things get bad for her—"

"Noah, stop fussing. I told you I'll be fine," Mrs. Cosgrove said. "I've got a nurse coming every day, and once I start feeling a bit better I'll be up and about, managing on my own."

Noah shoved his hand through his hair as if trying to corral his thoughts. Then he blew out a sigh that seemed to carry the weight of his reluctance. "Okay. I'll do it." He didn't sound very enthusiastic about it, but at that moment Shauntelle didn't care.

She would just have to find a way to work with Noah and keep her distance. Physically as well as emotionally.

"And that's our safety meeting for the day." Noah looked around the crew gathered at one end of the unfinished arena, his words echoing in the vast space. He sensed their boredom in the shifting postures and occasional glances at cell phones, which he would have preferred to prohibit completely. "I can't emphasize enough that a safe working environment is the most important thing."

It was Wednesday, the second day of him being in charge of the job site, and from the glances the crew exchanged, he could tell they were wondering if they had to deal with this every day.

Too bad. It was his responsibility to make sure they operated in a safe environment.

"Okay, you know what you should be working on, so let's get to it. And be careful," he added again. Just in case they didn't get the message the first couple of times.

They all dispersed, and Noah headed up to the area where the bleachers were being installed.

He was on the first step when someone called his name.

He stopped, confused at the way his heart jumped just a little as he turned to face Shauntelle, who was striding across the dirt floor of the arena, waving a blueprint. Her hair was pulled back and covered with a bandanna. She wore a plain white T-shirt tucked into blue jeans, and she looked fantastic.

She's not for you, he reminded himself.

Monday he'd spent the whole day with Kyle and Reuben Walsh, who had done the structural assessment. They went over the blueprints, making changes and assessing what to fix.

She came yesterday but he was off-site, dealing with an electrical supply company, and after that he had gone home to check on his mother. While he was there, he'd gotten a call from Kyle saying that Shauntelle wanted to talk to him, but when he came back to the site, she was picking up her daughters from school.

But today here she was, and she didn't look happy.

"I need to talk to you," she called out as she came nearer. "It's about the design you've changed."

Noah mentally shifted gears, wondering what changes she was referring to as he walked over to join her.

"What are you thinking?" she demanded, holding up the blueprint. "Making major changes without consulting me."

Noah caught the smirk of two younger employees and decided, from the anger on Shauntelle's face, to take care of this without an audience.

"Come into my office," he said, indicating the hall-

way leading to a room he'd taken over as his head-
quarters.

She looked like she wanted to get this taken care of
immediately, but he walked away. There was no way
she was confronting him in front of his crew.

He stood aside as she marched into his makeshift office, one of the future changing rooms, then dropped
the papers she was carrying on the old wooden table.
"Why did you change the entrance to the restaurant
without consulting me?"

So that was what this was about.

She smoothed out the blueprint she had with her, the
same one he'd been working from, and jabbed her finger
on part of it. "This was where we originally decided to
put the entrance. Why is it different?"

Noah moved closer to see why she was so upset. As
he did, he caught a whiff of her perfume. Light. Fruity.
He caught himself and focused on the papers.

"I had structural issues with the entrance's location,"
he said.

"Kyle said that you told him to move it. Why didn't
you talk to me first? Now they're going to knock a
hole in the wall in a different place." She faced him,
her eyes holding an anger that was out of proportion to
the issue at hand.

"Not until the end of the week. I tried calling last
night but you didn't answer your phone."

Shauntelle blinked, then turned away, looking flustered. "Well, I don't answer my phone when I'm with
my daughters or my…my family."

He heard her hesitation. He guessed her not answer-
ing his call had more to do with how her parents might
react to a call from him than spending quality time
with her family. For a moment he was tempted to throw

his hands up and walk away. Leave this job and Cedar Ridge. Her parents' feelings weren't changing, no matter how much he did to try to make amends.

But he had given his word, and his mother, in spite of her protestations, needed him.

"You being out of reach might prove problematic," Noah said, turning his attention back to her. "If we're working together and you want to be involved with this building project, I need to be able to get ahold of you."

"Send a text then" was her terse reply.

Right. Because texting was more unobtrusive and impersonal. He stifled another sigh. "I guess I can do that," he said. "As long as you reply as soon as possible."

"As soon as I can," she returned. "Now, talk to me about this entrance. What's wrong with where it was supposed to be initially?"

"If we put it where you want, we'll have to take a support out and I'm not compromising the integrity of that bearing wall. That's why I suggested what I did."

"But that's too far off in the corner. It's in a poor traffic area. People won't see it, or the snack bar. It will create a crowd in a corner, which will impact my business. That's why the previous contractor and I chose this spot."

"But the previous contractor isn't here now, is he?" That came out harsher than he meant. He could see from the way her eyes narrowed that she caught it as well.

"I used my own discretion when I decided to move it," Noah said.

Shauntelle pressed her lips together. He saw she was getting frustrated with him.

"I'm trying to make a go of this business. I'm competing with two other restaurants in town. I need every single advantage I can get," she said, her tone clipped.

Clearly she wasn't happy with him. Well, that wasn't anything new.

"And I'm trying to make sure the job site is safe for my workers as well as the building," he said. "Surely you should understand that."

He could tell his shot hit home from the look of shock on her face. As if he had mentioned the unmentionable.

But then, to his surprise, she held his gaze, her look assessing. As if she was trying to figure him out.

He didn't look away either, and he thought he glimpsed sorrow on her face. Then she glanced down.

He knew, however, that he couldn't ignore it. Whether he liked it or not, he needed to deal with the shadow of her brother's death—and Noah's involvement.

"I never gave you my condolences personally," he said, taking a chance, hoping it might ease the tension between them. "About your brother."

She turned on him, her eyes angry now. "No. You didn't. I noticed. So did my parents. We also noticed that you didn't come to the funeral." He shouldn't be surprised at her anger, since it likely stemmed from her grief and possibly the frustration of the change in her plans.

"Would you have wanted me there?" he returned, forcing himself to stay calm. To face her anger without getting pulled into the morass of guilt he'd fallen into after Josiah's death.

She didn't look away, but her eyes lost some of their snap and she shook her head. "Probably not."

He tapped his fingers on the blueprint, wishing he could find the right words to make her understand.

"Well, you need to know I think of him every day. Every day I regret what happened and wish I could change it," he said. He wanted to add that he hadn't been found to be at fault; however, that wouldn't change anything. Her brother had died working for him. That could never be erased.

She turned away, swallowing, and he wondered if she would cry.

But she pulled in a deep, slow breath, as if to compose herself, then turned back to him.

"That's good to know," she said, a small peace offering. "I appreciate you helping out. I don't know what we would have done if you hadn't."

"Put the door where I don't want it?"

She chuckled at that, and the sound was a gentle easing away of the momentary tension.

"I wish we could make this work," she said, resting her hands on her hips, frowning at the blueprint. "The building, that is. What if we change the opening? I had envisioned one large entrance with double glass doors. What if we keep it in the same place but switch it to two doors split by the support? It's not what I had planned, but if it means keeping the entrance where I want…"

Noah scratched his cheek with a forefinger, considering this. "I think that could work. I wouldn't be sacrificing the integrity of the building if we can keep that main support in place."

She chewed her lip, then bent over to look closer at the blueprint. As she did, her bandanna fell over her face.

Noah blamed his reaction on instinct. He reached over and gently pushed it back up on her head.

Her gaze flew to his, eyes wide, hands still holding on to the blueprint.

He saw her swallow, take a quick breath, then look away.

"Please don't do that again," she whispered, looking intently at the prints in her hand.

He said nothing, annoyed with himself but also with her overreaction. It was a simple thing. A tiny way of helping her.

Even if it had made his own heart flip and his breath quicken.

"Don't worry. I won't." He knew he had to keep his distance if he was going to get through the next couple months and leave fancy-free. He had no intention of getting involved with someone who would create so many complications.

Chapter Six

"Can we go out for supper tonight?" Millie shouted from the family room as soon as Shauntelle set foot inside her parents' house.

"Can you give me a minute to think?" she called back, slipping her laptop case off her shoulder and leaning against the door, catching her breath.

"Okay," came Millie's answer.

Thankfully, that seemed to be that.

Shauntelle was bone weary, and it was only Thursday. Today she had been in Calgary, dealing with the equipment supply place to arrange shipment, so she'd avoided Noah.

Wednesday evening she'd made the mistake of telling her parents what Noah said that day and regretted it. No sooner had she told them than her mother cried and her father got angry and left the room. The tension made her even more aware of Noah.

When he had so casually pushed her bandanna back on her head, she was unsettled at the shock his touch gave her. Her reaction made her feel pathetic, and yet, his gesture had been oddly endearing.

It touched a part of her that had been missing the

tender caring of a spouse. A partner. Her parents were still so lost in their grief and bitterness that they didn't have time to reach out. Shauntelle understood, but there were many times when she was grieving and lonely and longed for a hug or some human connection from someone who wanted to give. Not just take.

Margaret walked into the kitchen, followed by Millie. Both of them were grinning like they had something planned.

"What is going on?" she asked, her mom radar activating.

Millie feigned innocence. "We're hungry, and we haven't been out for ages and ages."

"Hardly ages," Shauntelle said, pushing herself away from the door. "And I'm sure Gramma made something for us to eat before they left for Calgary." She was surprised they'd gone to the city. Thankfully they had hired Nick Herbert, who worked part-time as a dishwasher at the Brand and Grill, to cover for them, so she couldn't begrudge them the time away. Right now she was relieved she didn't have to face her parents again.

Millie shook her head. "Nope. Nothing."

"Let me think about it," was all she would say, though making supper certainly had less appeal than the short drive to the café did.

"There's a super-great special on at the Brand and Grill," Margaret said, holding up the local paper. "Ribs and corn bread and lemon pie for dessert." She gave Shauntelle a sly smile. "We know how you love your lemon pie, and Mr. Muraski makes good lemon pie even if he is a grouch."

Shauntelle grinned at Margaret's comment. "I like lemon pie."

"So we can go?" Millie pressed.

Shauntelle glanced over at the kitchen. The thought of making supper was simply too much for her. "Sure. That sounds good."

And before she could get another word out, they grabbed their spring jackets and were out the door, giggling. She followed, stifling the vague sense that something was afoot, then brushed it aside. She couldn't keep up with her daughters these days. Far easier to just go with the flow.

They climbed in, buckled up and were whispering, heads bent together, when Shauntelle got back in the vehicle.

"So how long are we going to be using Gramma's car?" Millie asked.

"I don't know, honey." She had so many other things to juggle, and a vehicle was far down the list. "Why do you ask?"

"Grandpa was asking Gramma how long you would use it, and Gramma said it was up to her and to leave her alone. Then Grandpa said it was bad enough you are working with that evil man but you using her car to do it made it worse."

Shauntelle's hands clenched the steering wheel as she headed down the street, fighting down guilt, anger and hurt. Why would her father say that? The girls overhearing was not his fault. They were like little spies, sneaking about, catching whatever tidbits of information they could, without realizing the import of what they passed on.

But the result was strain on a relationship that was already heavy with grief and loss and proximity—and the added stress of her working with Noah every day.

Help me deal with this all, Lord, she prayed, struggling with her latent sorrow. *Help me to lean on You.*

She pulled in a slow breath, as if to let the prayer settle. She glimpsed her smiling daughters in her rear-view mirror, happy with the unexpected outing. In this moment, things were okay, she reminded herself. *Hold on to that.*

She got out of the car just as the girls piled out, chattering their excitement about this special treat.

"Can we order ice cream with sprinkles?" Millie asked as she held open the door for Shauntelle.

"I think that's a possibility," Shauntelle said, smiling at her precocious daughter, thankful for this unexpected one-on-one time with the twins.

"I want nuts on mine," Margaret said. "Our teacher told us yesterday that nuts are healthy."

"But ice cream isn't healthy, so it doesn't matter," Millie, her daughter with an answer for everything, shot back.

Adana, a tall, slim girl with cropped dark hair, greeted them with a vague smile and a languid flip of her hand. "Just sit wherever," she said as she dropped menus into the holder. "I got an order to run."

"I know where I want to sit," Millie said, and charged ahead, Margaret right behind her.

Shauntelle followed them, then stifled a groan. Just her luck.

The girls sat at a table with Noah and his mother. And from the way Millie and Margaret were chatting with them, she suspected this was part of some plan they had concocted. The worst part was, she knew there was no way out.

This had to be a setup.

Noah looked from Shauntelle's ticked-off expression to the giggling girls sitting at the table right beside him and his mother. The three chatted like old friends, and Shauntelle didn't look pleased.

Well, neither was he.

He had wondered why his mother had been so insistent that they eat out tonight. She told him it was so he didn't have to cook, but he had pulled out a couple of chicken breasts this morning and bought potatoes and vegetables at the store, so he was prepared.

Now, as his mother smiled her welcome at Shauntelle, he guessed something else was up. Especially since she asked him every day how Shauntelle was, commenting on what a lovely girl she was and how adorable her daughters were. And wasn't she simply the best cook, she had asked after they had finished one of her meat pies.

Subtle and *mother* were not words he put together very often.

"Well, well, here you are," his mother said with a huge smile. "Funny we should meet you and your adorable daughters here."

Funny indeed. His mother and her daughters were up to something.

"Yes, that's quite a coincidence," he said with a wry tone, looking over at his mother. But she didn't look at him at all.

"Guess we all had the same idea," his mother said, turning back to the girls.

"Or something like that," Shauntelle returned, hesitating by the table. Noah guessed she would make one last-ditch effort to separate her daughters from his mother, but from the way they were chatting like long-lost buddies, that probably wasn't happening.

She seemed to realize that too and finally sat down.

"Mrs. Cosgrove was telling us about her horses,"

Millie piped up as Shauntelle hooked her purse over the back of the chair. "She said we should come over and ride them."

Noah nudged his mother under the table. She shot him a frown, and then looked away. "They haven't been ridden in a while. I know it would be great for them to get some exercise," his mother said, her gaze bobbing between Shauntelle and her avid audience of two.

"I don't know if that's such a good idea," Noah added, giving both her and him an out. "Like you said, Mom, no one's ridden them in a while, and I doubt Millie and Margaret have ever been on a horse."

His mother waved off his protests. "Those horses are as old as Methuselah. The girls would be perfectly safe on them."

"And we would be really careful," Margaret put in, eyes wide as if to underline her sincerity. "Really, really careful."

"Super, super careful," Millie added.

"And super careful is far more careful than really careful," Noah said with a grin, unable to stop himself from teasing them.

He caught Shauntelle glancing over at him, and as their eyes met, he saw a smile playing over her lips and a twinkle in her eye. Clearly she had the same difficulty staying serious that he did.

"So why don't you bring the girls over on Saturday?" his mother asked, pressing the point.

"Please, Mom. Please," the twins chimed in. "Please, pretty please."

"I have Farmer's Market," she said.

"You can come after that," Mrs. Cosgrove put in.

"Please," the girls added, in case she didn't get the first four.

"We haven't asked Mr. Cosgrove yet," Shauntelle said.

Noah shot her a warning frown. "So you're putting this on me?"

"The ball is in your court. You'll have to play it out."

Perfect, he thought, turning to face wide, expectant blue eyes and blazing smiles, their adorableness quotient more than doubling.

"We'll see," was all he could manage.

The girls erupted into cheers that made everyone in the restaurant glance over their way. What were the girls celebrating? He had said nothing definite.

"Girls. Quiet," Shauntelle warned. "Mr. Cosgrove didn't say yes. He just said that he would see."

"But 'we'll see' is closer to yes than no," Millie said.

Noah couldn't help a faint snort, which he immediately covered up with a napkin.

"That is excellent," his mother said, clearly coming to the same conclusion the girls did. "Shauntelle can bring the girls to the ranch after the Farmer's Market."

Just then, Adana came over and handed them each a menu before Noah could protest.

"Anything to drink?" she asked.

"Chocolate milk," the girls said, then glanced over at Shauntelle. "If that's okay?"

"Chocolate milk is a bit more expensive, girls," Shauntelle said.

"It's fine," Noah put in, nodding at Adana. "And one bill. To me."

"No. I'll pay for us," Shauntelle protested.

Noah shook his head, giving her a teasing smile. "If the ball is in my court, you should let me play it out," he said.

"You don't need to feel… I mean, we barged in—"

"Please. Don't worry about it." Then, just to ease

the concern on her face he leaned closer, lowering his voice. "And just to keep things on the up-and-up, I had nothing to do with this little meeting today."

No sooner had he spoken the words than he felt like smacking his head. What if she wasn't even thinking this might have been a setup?

Shauntelle's gaze flicked from his mother to her daughters, then back to him, a surprising touch of humor in her voice. "I'm sure this was my daughters' doing."

Noah nodded, feeling a surprising relief at her smile. "Well, I wouldn't leave my mother out of the mix. I'm sure she was involved too. I know you'll be tired after the Farmer's Market," he said, giving her an out. "If you don't want to come on Saturday, I understand."

She cut him off with a wave of her hand and a look of feigned horror. "There's no way I'm telling the girls that now."

He laughed at that, and for a moment their eyes held and it seemed as if everything else faded away. His breath caught in his chest, and as his heart lifted, he caught himself unsettled by the feelings she created in him.

Allowing himself to feel anything at all for someone like Shauntelle was problematic.

And too risky. But as he looked over at the excited girls and the animation on his mother's face, he knew he couldn't stop what they were planning.

He would let them come and ride horses, but he really had to keep his distance.

Shauntelle and her daughters were an emotional entanglement he couldn't allow in his life.

Chapter Seven

"I don't think you should take those girls to the Cosgrove ranch tomorrow." Shauntelle's mother leaned back against the counter, her arms crossed over her chest, her body language hostile.

Shauntelle turned the toaster upside down and shook the bread crumbs into the sink. Weariness washed over her, and for a moment she was tempted to give in to her mother's not-so-subtle hints. Ever since her parents found out about her plans, Shauntelle had put up with frowns, covert comments and strong pushback.

"I told the girls they could." She knew her parents would be upset by this new turn of events, but she also knew if she told Millie and Margaret they couldn't go, they would rebel. Big-time.

All the way back from the café, they had chattered about what they would wear when they went riding and whether they would be afraid to gallop the horses or not.

Shauntelle had let them talk, still trying to deal with her own shifting feelings for Noah. It would be so much easier to give in to her mother's wishes than to face Noah again and try to figure out what to do with the emotions he fostered in her.

In that moment in the café, when Noah had held her gaze, an undercurrent of awareness had buzzed through her that she knew was a major distraction. There was no way she would be sidetracked from the plans she had poured so much into.

Besides, he came with so much history.

"It's so wrong," her mother said, a plaintive note entering her voice.

Shauntelle gripped the toaster, her eyes locked on the window as she dealt with conflicting feelings. Her gaze slid sideways and latched onto a group of pictures sitting on the windowsill. Her brother on his motorbike. Another one of her and Josiah when they were in high school. Josiah laughing with his friends, and a fourth one of him with his arms spread out, a huge grin on his face. That one was taken just before he jumped off a bridge attached to a bungee cord.

And these were only a few of the many pictures her parents had put up around the house after Josiah died. As if they needed reminders everywhere of what they lost.

She stared at the picture of her brother, grief beating through her. She thought of the plans they had made together. This restaurant she was working on was supposed to be both of theirs. It had been a dream they had nurtured together. The months when Roger worked overseas or the evenings he was at the hospital, Josiah would come over and they would draw up plans, make up menus. It was a bright spot for Shauntelle. A place where she felt like she had control.

Then Roger died. Josiah waited two months, then told Shauntelle that he had changed his mind. He didn't want to live a tame life. He wanted to travel. He sold his truck, broke up with his girlfriend and headed out.

He went extreme skiing in Peru, surfing in Indonesia, backpacking in Nepal and taking risks along the way. When he came back, he needed to pay off his loans, so he started working for Noah.

Then he died.

It was as if Shauntelle was being told over and over again that she couldn't count on anyone. It was up to her to take care of herself and her daughters.

"If you wanted to take the girls out you could have asked us," her mother said. "We could have done something with them instead of you taking them…over there."

Again she heard the undercurrent. Noah wasn't worthy.

She felt like a traitor to her brother's memory and her parents' grief.

And she felt an unwelcome twist of frustration as she pushed the breakfast tray into the cupboard. "It's not like you and Dad have time," she said. "And I don't always have the energy or the money."

"Well, maybe we could make time," her mother offered.

"Maybe you could and that would be nice, but for now I made this promise to them and I can't see how I can break it." Shauntelle gave her mother a gentle smile, torn between her daughters' wishes and her mother's sorrow.

Her mother held her steady gaze, then looked away, her mouth trembling. "Okay. I understand. I see what's happening."

It wasn't too hard to hear the disappointment in her voice, but at this moment Shauntelle was ready to give her girls a break from the heaviness in this household and the constant guilt her mother was piling on her.

She kissed her mother and put her hand on her shoulder. "I love you, Mom," she said, her small peace offering. Thankfully her mother smiled back.

"I love you too. Hope that your…work…your plans… that they go well today."

Her hesitancy to even speak Noah's name was a vivid reminder of her mother's opinion of him.

"Do you need me to come and get you later today?" Shauntelle asked, moving along to more practical matters. "So that you can help Dad?"

"I have to work on the books today. Nick is coming to help your dad today. Sepp isn't giving him as many hours at the café, so we told him he could come work for us." Then her mother gave her a gentle smile and left.

Shauntelle eased out a sigh, grabbed her lunch bag and headed to the car.

As she drove from the house to the arena, she felt a shift from the burdens her parents wanted her to carry and the reality of the tension of working with Noah. He was attractive and appealing—and a huge complication. He would drive a wedge between her and her parents.

And she owed them too much to hurt them like that.

Lord, I'm so tired, she prayed. *I wish I could find some rest.*

The quick prayer was all she could manage as her mind sorted through her day. The company she was purchasing the kitchen equipment from was coming to do some measurements. The crew was working on the entrance to the main restaurant today, and she wanted to be around. She had to pick up the girls from school, and then bake for Farmer's Market and find time to get her laundry done. She got tired just thinking of all that needed to be done today.

Focus on the page in front of you. Turn the page and do the next thing.

These words had served her well after Roger died and she couldn't handle all the information tossed at her. She was grieving and upset and lost. She bought a scribbler and on each page wrote one task. Then she prayed, turned the page and dealt with the very next thing. This narrowed her choices and helped her focus when things grew overwhelming.

By the time she walked into the arena, nail guns pounded, saws buzzed and generators hummed. The twang of country music echoed through the large open space, as well as the beeping of a reversing man lift. The place was a beehive of activity.

She skirted a group of carpenters looking over some plans and a pile of lumber stacked in a walkway as she made her way around the arena to the part where her restaurant would be.

Yesterday they were starting on the opening, and she was excited to see what had happened since then. She had special ordered the doors, and they—along with the installers—were coming Monday.

But when she stepped into the foyer, it was empty. No one was working and, even worse, a large expanse of unbroken wall where the door was supposed to be faced her.

What was going on? Noah knew the doors were coming. Why weren't the guys working on the opening?

Just then Kyle Wierenga, the foreman, came through the foyer doors whistling, clearly pleased with how things were going on-site.

"Hey, girlie, how are you doing?" he asked, giving her a broad smile.

"Not well at all." She put heavy emphasis on every

word, waving her hand at the wall behind her. "Where is the opening for my door? Noah promised it would be done. I've got the order coming in on Monday, and now there's no hole for them to put them in. They need to be installed as soon as they arrive, and if they can't be, the workers will have to wait until they can or bring them back. I can't afford to pay for either option."

She heard her shrill voice reverberating through the empty foyer, volume growing with each sentence, and from the look on Kyle's face he was wondering when she would come at him with claws bared.

"I'll get Noah," Kyle said, backing away like he would from a wounded cougar.

She pressed her lips together, ashamed of her actions. She didn't know if it was the confrontation with her mother this morning, the fight she'd had with Millie over a filthy pair of pants she insisted on wearing, her struggle with needing to work with Noah and her parents' disapproval, or just exhaustion in general, but suddenly she was overwhelmed.

A knot of very unwelcome tears thickened her throat and she leaned against the wall, her hands covering her face.

Please, Lord.

"Shauntelle?"

She sucked in a couple of quick breaths, trying to get her grief under control, then turned to face Noah.

"Is something wrong?" His frown pulled his dark eyebrows together, hardening his expression. "Kyle said you were angry about the door."

"Or the lack thereof," she said, crossing her arms over her chest.

"The opening is going in Monday. As we had

agreed." He moved closer, his frown deepening, which made him look even less approachable.

"No. We said today. My doors are coming in Monday." Again, that shrill note slipped into her voice.

He shook his head, pulling out his phone and tapping the screen. "I've got a note here that says we're doing it Monday. We can double-check the schedule. It's in my office."

Noah's voice took on a conciliatory, patronizing tone. The same one, she realized, that she used when her kids were being especially annoying.

"Let's do that." She spun around, striding away from him to his office, one part of her brain telling her to relax, the other whirling into a vortex of uncontrollable emotions.

Noah's footsteps echoed behind her, and when they got to the office, he was right behind her. He closed the door after entering. Probably to make sure any tantrum she threw wouldn't be heard by his workers.

He was annoyingly calm as he pulled out his laptop where he kept all the records of what was supposed to happen when. He tapped and typed, then turned it around to show her a large spreadsheet. "See? It's here. Monday."

She frowned at the screen, still not sure she was in the wrong. "Then why would I have ordered my doors for Monday?"

"Maybe you got the start date mixed up with the delivery date."

Shauntelle just stared at the laptop, biting her lip, still not sure what to think.

"You know how meticulous I am about my schedules," he continued. "I can't afford to mess things up. I'm on a tight schedule and things need to move smoothly. Especially after…" He stopped there, and Shauntelle guessed where he was going.

After Josiah's death.

She rested her hands on the table in front, the anger wilting out of her as she adjusted her thinking. The doors would arrive Monday, and the crew couldn't install them until the next day. She would have to pay time and a half and any other expenses incurred by the crew if there were delays. The doors were already over her budget, and now they would cost her more because she had misunderstood.

She closed her eyes, suddenly overwhelmed by everything crowding in on her.

Her throat thickened, and behind that came panic. No. She couldn't cry. Not now.

She went to turn away, her head down. But as she did, the corner of her sweater caught the table. She yanked at it and then, to her horror, Noah's laptop slid over, then tipped off the edge and onto the ground.

"Oh no!" she cried, trying to catch it, but it fell with a sickening smack on the cement. The screen cracked and the display went dead. "I'm so sorry," she said, kneeling down to pick it up.

"Don't worry," he said, coming around the table, getting down as well. She stared at his frowning face, his deep-set eyes looking concerned.

And suddenly it was all too much.

The tears she had been fighting slid down her cheeks; the sobs she'd been swallowing now crawled up her throat. She pulled her knees up to her chest, glaring at Noah.

"I can't do this anymore," she whispered, balling her hands into fists. "It's too much. My brother, my mom and dad, my kids. Those stupid doors." She choked on those last words, then dropped her head on her knees and fought the sorrow that threatened to swamp her.

Too much. Too much.

Then Noah was beside her, his arm around her shoulder, and she leaned into him and gave in to her emotions.

She knew she should stop, but the dam had burst.

It all washed over her, pulling her along, and all the while she was aware of Noah holding her close.

"It's okay," he murmured as he held her to him, his head pressed on top of hers. "I understand. You don't have to carry it all."

Watch out.

The tiny voice of reason whispered behind the comfort of Noah's arms. She should pay attention, but she was bone weary. Tired of holding everything up herself. Having Noah's arms around her, dangerous as it might be, felt good for now.

So she laid her head against his chest, hearing the steady thump of his heart, inhaling the scent of wood mixed with soap and the faint scent of his spicy aftershave. She pulled in a deep breath, surprised when his arms tightened around her.

They sat that way a moment longer, and then she pulled back, feeling a need to see his face. Wondering what she would see in his deep brown eyes.

He looked so serious. Then his hand came up, and he eased a strand of hair back from her face, his fingers brushing over her skin.

Then his hand cupped her face, and he bent his head and brushed his lips over hers. Then, before she even realized what she was doing, her hand was on his cheek, her thumb tracing his strong jawline, and she returned his kiss. His lips were warm, welcoming, and she felt as if she had come home.

Moments later, she drew back, wondering why she didn't feel bad about what had just happened.

"Shauntelle…" His voice trailed off, as if saying her name was all he could do.

Their eyes held, gazes locked as she tried to read his expression, delve into his soul.

"I wish I didn't have to have my hair in silly braids," Millie said, giving her head a shake, her braids bouncing on her shoulders. "I want to have my hair flowing behind me in the wind. I want to feel like Merida."

"Merida has red hair," Margaret corrected her. "Your hair is yellow."

Millie ignored her practical sister, her dreamy smile showing Shauntelle that she was off in another world. Probably galloping on a horse.

The girls had been crazy all morning. Shauntelle blamed it on her own bemusement. She couldn't count how many times she'd relived that moment when Noah had kissed her. Every time she did, a flush touched her cheeks and a curious warmth filled her heart.

The whole time she had been working her booth at the Farmer's Market, she had struggled not to check her watch or her phone. This morning Noah had texted her asking if she still wanted to come. She had written him a text, saying yes, yet her finger hovered over the send key. Again she thought of her parents, and again she realized that no matter what she did, it would be wrong. It was time she put herself and her daughters first.

Besides, there was no way she would get away with telling the girls they weren't going.

So she hid behind their happiness, tucking away her own anticipation and apprehension.

She turned on the road, driving past the spot where she had first met Noah, her mind slipping back to that encounter.

"Here's where our car broke down," Millie said, her comment echoing Shauntelle's thoughts. "I'm so glad Mr. Noah could rescue us. He's so handsome."

Shauntelle couldn't help the quick skip of her own heart. But she didn't acknowledge her daughter's comment as she drove on.

"Here we are," Millie called out a few moments later as Shauntelle turned down the driveway of the T Bar C. She unbuckled and leaned over the seat, almost panting with excitement. Shauntelle was about to reprimand her, but she wasn't going that fast, and Millie was too excited.

"Look, there's Mr. Noah with the horses!" Millie shouted, her finger jabbing past Shauntelle's head. "I'm so excited."

"You have to sit down until we're stopped," Margaret said, her voice prim. But Shauntelle could hear she was just as excited as her sister.

Shauntelle parked where she had when she and the girls dropped the baking off the other day. No sooner had she turned the engine off than her daughters were out of the car and racing toward the corral.

"You girls wait up for me!" Shauntelle called out, hurrying to catch up to them.

But they were too giddy, and they ignored her. Thankfully they didn't clamber over the corral fence and were content to just stand on the bottom rail, their arms perched over the top as they watched Noah tie up the horses.

He wore a cowboy hat today, a twill shirt rolled up over his forearms tucked into snug blue jeans, and worn cowboy boots. He looked comfortable, self-confident, and against the background of the corrals, the pastures and the mountains behind him, he fit in perfectly.

"So are you girls ready to go riding?" he asked as he came nearer.

"We are so excited," Millie called out, bouncing on the lower rail of the fence.

"Are we galloping?" Margaret asked, sounding fearful.

Noah chuckled and shook his head. "I know you girls are excited, but right now we're just walking."

"Out in the pastures, in the open fields?" Millie asked.

"We'll just start in the corrals for now," Noah said, smiling as Millie's mouth turned down, expressing her disappointment. He glanced over at Shauntelle. Their eyes held a second longer than they should, but she didn't want to look away.

The memory of the kiss they had shared rose and altered everything between them. She knew they couldn't go back. However, all she saw ahead were questions of how this could work. She had no room for a relationship, and Noah was the last person she should consider dating.

Losing Roger had pulled the ground out from under her emotionally and mentally. It had taken her this long to find her way again. To create her own life. Did she dare allow herself to depend on anyone again?

"How are you doing?" he asked with concern.

"About what?"

"The doors?"

"I'll manage," she said, his concern touching her. It

had been a long time since anyone besides her parents cared what happened to her.

"Which horse am I going to ride?" Millie asked, her loud voice reminding Shauntelle why they were here. And it wasn't to flirt with Noah.

"I thought I would give you the palomino and Margaret the brown horse," Noah said, dragging his gaze away from her.

The girls looked at the horses then at each other, as if they had to confer. Then they both nodded. "That will work for us."

"We're so glad you approve," Shauntelle teased.

"That's all I can hope for," Noah said, adding a grin.

Once again she couldn't look away. Once again she felt as if the walls she had built around her heart were being breached.

"So can we go on the horses?" Millie asked, crossing one leg over the fence, ready to take off.

"Yes, but I need to warn you girls you have to be quiet around the horses and that you have to move slowly," Noah said.

Shauntelle couldn't help a faint shiver of concern as she grabbed her daughters' hands to make sure they followed Noah's instructions. Those creatures were huge. "So these horses are okay?"

Millie and Margaret were pulling on her hands, but she held them back.

"I can guarantee they're quiet. I rode the horses out last night, just to make sure."

Shauntelle shot him a curious look. "You took the time to ride them already? Both of them?"

"Of course I did." He almost sounded offended.

"I'm sorry. I guess… I'm just surprised."

"I'm a cautious person. I want you to know that."

He had his hands in his pockets, his shoulders hunched forward as his eyes seemed to drill into her, underlining what he was saying.

She held his defensive gaze and gave him another smile, even as the girls tugged at her hands. "I know what you're saying. And I trust you."

He seemed to relax at that, and another smile curved his lips. And another shiver teased Shauntelle's vulnerable heart.

"I want to ride," Millie said, still tugging on Shauntelle's hands.

"First, we have to introduce you." Noah turned his attention to the girls. "Margaret, you come with me."

Shauntelle was pleased that he chose Margaret first. Millie, with her outspoken and dominant nature, tended to get the most attention. Shauntelle could see from the way she pouted that she wasn't used to this order of events. Shauntelle gave Millie's hand an extra squeeze of warning, to ensure she didn't complain.

Noah made Margaret stroke the horse and showed her how to walk around him, letting the animal know where she was by talking and touching it. Noah was patient and took his time. Margaret's grin almost split her face; she was so excited at the attention and at being close to the horse. After he had gone over some basic horse sense, he picked her up and set her in the saddle.

"This is how you hold on to the saddle horn," he said, demonstrating.

"I'm not steering the horse myself?"

"Nope. Not this time."

"Okay."

"Are you going to be alright up there?" he asked, his hand resting on the horse's neck, his other on his hip as he looked up at her.

Margaret just nodded. She looked happier than she had in months. Which, for Shauntelle, showed her that she had made the right choice in coming here.

"You want to come and join us?" Noah gestured for Millie to come forward.

Millie didn't need any more urging than that, and ran toward Noah and the horses.

"Whoa. Stop right there." Noah took a quick step toward her and held his hands up. "Remember what I said about moving slow."

Millie stopped where she was and hung her head. "I'm sorry. I forgot because I was so excited."

Noah crouched down in front of her, one hand on her shoulder. "It's okay. I know you're excited. But you have to be very attentive around horses."

Millie just nodded. Then Noah held his hand out to her. She slipped it in his and he walked toward the horses. He went through the same routine he had with Margaret. Soon both girls were astride the horses, and Noah was untying the reins from the fence. He clucked to the horses and, with a set of reins in each hand, led them around the corrals.

"He's very careful, isn't he?"

Noah's mother had spoken quietly, but her unexpected presence still made Shauntelle jump.

She glanced over at Mrs. Cosgrove, who was now standing beside her, leaning on her crutches. She looked less pale today, and she was smiling as she always did.

"He said he rode the horses last night to settle them down for today." Fay Cosgrove looked over, and in her eyes Shauntelle caught the same intensity she saw in Noah. "He's a good man. He can come across as difficult, but he's got a good heart."

Shauntelle heard something other than a mother's

pride in her son as Mrs. Cosgrove spoke. It was as if she was trying to convince Shauntelle of Noah's goodness.

She wanted to reply but was afraid that anything she would say would reveal the uncertain feelings Noah created in her. So she simply smiled and looked back at the corral where Noah was leading her daughters around. "I'm thankful he's willing to do this for my daughters."

"Oh, I don't think he's doing it just for them." This was followed by a meaningful glance her way.

Shauntelle felt a flush warm her neck, but right then the girls on their horses came past, giving her an excuse not to answer. She waved at the girls, trying to keep her eyes off Noah.

"I'm pretending I'm on a bucking bronc," Millie called out and lifted her arm. When Noah shot her a warning glance, to Shauntelle's surprise and pleasure, her daughter immediately settled down.

"Hi, Mrs. Cosgrove," Millie called out. "Look at us. We're riding."

"You look like you were born on a horse," Mrs. Cosgrove said with a grin. "When you're done, you should come to the house for something to drink and some cookies."

"Chocolate chip?" Margaret asked.

"Is there any other kind?" Mrs. Cosgrove asked.

The girls laughed as they turned their attention back to the horses.

"Your daughter Millie is quite the character, isn't she?" Mrs. Cosgrove said as Millie became more subdued.

"She's always testing me." Shauntelle laid her arms on the sun-warmed fence, shaking her head as she watched her daughter. "Especially since…since Roger died."

"I'm guessing she has a strong will?"

"A mighty will," Shauntelle added. "When Roger was alive he could keep her in check. But since then…" Her voice trailed off, and it was as if she was hearing her own words for the first time. Like articulating her thoughts in front of Mrs. Cosgrove made her realize what was going on with her daughter.

"I think she needs a strong hand in her life," Mrs. Cosgrove said.

Shauntelle realized the truth in what she was saying. And her eyes slid again to Noah, who was chatting with the girls as he led them around the corral. He seemed very comfortable with them. And he wasn't intimidated by Millie, which was more than she could say for her father. He never seemed to know what to do with the girls.

"I'm sure it's been difficult raising the girls on your own," Fay said. "I'm sure you still miss your husband."

Shauntelle lifted one shoulder and gave a slight shrug, not sure what to say. "Of course I miss him," she said. "But he wasn't around much even when he was alive. He was a very dedicated doctor and often stayed late at night to work. And then when he got on with Doctors Without Borders, he would be gone weeks at a time." She stopped there, realizing that she was sounding whiny. "He was a good man too," she said. "A very good husband and father."

"I know your parents were very proud of him." Mrs. Cosgrove also looked over at Noah and shifted her weight on her crutches. "I understand that pride. I'm proud of my son too, and I also love him dearly." She stopped there, easing out a sigh. "You need to know how sorry I feel for your parents. Losing their only son and their son-in-law was a terrible blow for them."

Then Mrs. Cosgrove put her hand on Shauntelle's arm and squeezed. "Please know that I don't want to minimize their loss, but I wish you could let them know my son did everything he could to make sure Josiah was safe. Noah doesn't like it when I talk about this, but I want you to know that he feels horrible about the accident. He always says he should have spent more time training him. Being there for your brother. He takes it very personally, even though it has been proven that he wasn't at fault."

Shauntelle allowed herself a moment to gather her own confused thoughts, trying to sort out her feelings about her brother, her parents.

Noah.

"Your son told me the same," she said, giving Mrs. Cosgrove a shy look, feeling self-conscious about saying his name around his mother. Like a teen girl talking about her crush. "He told me that not a day goes by that he doesn't wish things could have gone differently. That he doesn't wonder what else he could have done." She paused a moment, wondering if she should say what had been hovering on the edges of any memory of Josiah's accident. That Noah had less to do with what happened than Josiah did.

"But I believe there's two sides to this story," Shauntelle continued, as memories of the pictures her parents had of her brother floated to the surface. Josiah bungee jumping, racing on his motorbike, hang gliding. And as they did, other memories returned. Other realities. "I think Josiah always was a risk taker," she said, her thoughts taking shape as she spoke. "I remember him saying fear was for the fearful, whatever that was supposed to mean. I think he thought it made him sound tough. Unafraid." She stopped there, feeling like a traitor to her brother's memory and her parents' grief.

However, she knew what she had revealed was the other truth about her brother's life. And by talking about him to Mrs. Cosgrove, she could step back from the situation and see her brother through different eyes. Think of him from a different point of view than her grieving and bitter parents did.

"I don't think Noah was as much to blame as he seems to think he is." And in that moment, as the words spilled out of her, she heard the truth in them. Felt a sense of relief. Of a burden shifting off her shoulders.

"Thank you for saying that," Mrs. Cosgrove whispered. "I have always felt that, but I also know I'm biased when it comes to my son. I never wanted your parents to feel I was diminishing their loss, but it was also my son who had to deal with a lot. I've seen people glancing away from me, heard conversations stop when I come into the café or into church. That hasn't been easy either. To think that people thought less of my son."

Shauntelle heard the pain in Mrs. Cosgrove's voice. At that moment, she realized that while her parents had suffered a huge loss, Fay Cosgrove had her own sorrows to deal with as well.

As had Noah.

Her eyes followed him as he led her daughters around, chatting easily with them. He seemed at ease and, she realized, he was smiling. A real, genuine smile. Something she hadn't seen since she met him. In fact, thinking back, she never saw him smile much when she knew him in school.

"I hope I'm not making you uncomfortable," Mrs. Cosgrove said, misinterpreting her silence.

"No. Not at all," Shauntelle said, turning to her and

covering her hand with her own in a gesture of assurance. "I guess I never realized the repercussions for you and Noah."

"Noah has had a hard life and…well…his father was a difficult and demanding person. I should have been there more for him." Her regret clearly came through.

"I'm sorry to hear that." She was also surprised. She had always thought Noah Cosgrove was one of the lucky ones.

"I am too." Then Fay gave her a melancholy look. "And I'm sorry to have taken over the conversation. You've lost a lot more than I ever have."

Shauntelle acknowledged her sympathy with a nod, then gave her another smile. "It's been hard, but to tell you the truth, I'm getting ready to move on."

"That's good to know."

Fay Cosgrove's voice held a curious tone—and was that a glint in her eyes?

"Look, Mom, I'm riding a horse!" Margaret called out to her as they rode past, breaking into the moment. "And Mr. Noah says I'm doing really good."

"You're just sitting there," Millie returned, but this time Margaret didn't rise to the bait Millie always dangled in front of her sister.

"You're both doing well," Noah put in, his eyes catching Shauntelle's.

For a moment, neither of them looked away as he walked past her, but then one horse flicked its head up and his attention was back on the girls.

Shauntelle watched as they made another long circle, smiling. Her girls were happy. The sun was warm on her head, granting the promise of warmer temperatures and longer days. Today was a good day.

And then as he turned, Noah looked over at her again, their eyes locked and Shauntelle's heart lifted.

Possibilities swirled. Hope sparked. A kiss was remembered.

Did she dare allow herself this tiny dream? This distraction?

Chapter Eight

"Do you want to take a turn?" Noah asked Shauntelle.

"I'm fine," Shauntelle said, shooting a quick glance at her watch. He wondered what she was checking for.

The ride was over, and she had joined him and the girls. As he lifted them out of the saddle, he told them they had to help him.

And now Shauntelle stood beside him, showing the twins how to hold the bridle and wrap the reins so they didn't tangle.

"You know something about horse tack?" he asked, surprised.

"I've ridden before," she said, giving him a slight grin. "Enough of my friends lived on ranches or acreages that I've been out on a horse several times."

He held her gaze, and in spite of the girls there, his mind cast back to the kiss they had shared yesterday. And right now he wanted to do it again. He wished he could blame his reaction on plain, ordinary loneliness, but he knew there was more going on between them. Feelings he hadn't experienced in a long time. A sense of rightness he never had with his former fiancée.

She's staying.

You're leaving.
You're the Evil Man.
She returned my kiss.

"How did the Farmer's Market go this morning?" Noah asked.

"Pretty good."

"We didn't have as much because Mom was so mixed-up yesterday. She kept making mistakes. She even had to throw out a whole batch of muffins." Millie gave Noah a knowing look. "Too much baking powder. That happens sometimes."

Noah chuckled.

"I wasn't mixed-up," Shauntelle protested, shooting a frown at Millie.

"Yes you were," Margaret put in, coiling up the reins like Shauntelle had shown her. "You were just staring out the window a bunch of times and you almost burned the cakes."

He would not look at her. He wasn't assuming that what happened between them had anything to do with her distraction.

But in spite of his self-talk, he stole a glance, surprised to see her cheeks flushed and her gaze averted.

"And then my mom got a phone call from someone named Ella. She wants some baking for her wedding." Millie toyed with the reins, slowly looping them around her hand as she looked over at Noah. "Do you know her? She's marrying Cord Walsh. His boy, Paul, is in our class in school and he's so excited that he will get a mom. Lucky him."

"You have a mom," Noah said, loosening the cinch strap.

"But we don't have a dad."

There was no way Noah was going within sniffing distance of that comment.

"Can you please put the bridle away, missy?" he said instead.

"It's Millie," she corrected, sounding huffy.

"Excuse me," Shauntelle said, tapping her daughter on the shoulder. "Manners."

"I'm sorry, Mr. Noah, but my name is Millie."

"I know. I think you should be called Missy, Millie." Noah shot her a teasing glance, and she accepted his comment with another nod.

"That sounds good."

"Glad you approve. Now can you put the bridle away?"

Thankfully she didn't give him any attitude after that and flounced off, her braids bobbing behind her.

"I'm so sorry about that," Shauntelle said. "She's been in a mood all morning."

Noah held up a hand, chuckling. "No worries. She's a pistol, that one. I'm thinking you have to fight hard to keep up with her."

Shauntelle sighed. "You're right. It's a steady and exhausting battle of wills. She needs a firmer hand than I can give her sometimes."

"Probably needs a male role model in her life."

No sooner had he said that than he wished he hadn't. It didn't come out as he'd intended.

"I guess I meant to say that I'm sure she misses her father." He stopped himself there, realizing that anything he would add to that would only dig him in deeper.

"We hung up the bridles," Margaret said as the girls rejoined them. Their timing saved him from making a bigger fool of himself.

"Just let me get the saddles off, and you can bring the blankets to the tack shed."

"Can we come again on Monday?" Millie asked as he released the cinch.

"I'm not sure," Noah said. And that's all he would say to that. He enjoyed being around the girls; they were a lot of fun. But he didn't know if he should spend extra time with this small family on purpose.

"That's good enough for me," Millie said with the confidence that seemed to belie the vagueness of his comment.

A few moments later he had the saddles off and he followed the girls to the tack shed. They chattered away as he showed them how to lay the blankets out so they could dry, and set the saddles on their stands. He fussed around a bit, straightening halters, adjusting the saddles, reluctant to return to Shauntelle.

But the girls flounced out ahead of him, and he followed.

"Can we go see your mom?" Millie asked. "She was here while we were riding but now she's gone. We didn't have time to talk to her."

"I think Mrs. Cosgrove is tired," Shauntelle said. "I don't want to bother her."

"But she invited us to come in," Millie wailed, turning to Shauntelle and putting on what Noah thought must be her most plaintive look.

Shauntelle bit her lip, looking uncertain. He wasn't ready for them to go home either. He enjoyed spending time with the girls, and if he was honest, the chance for some social time with Shauntelle was even more appealing.

Then his mother was on the porch, calling out to the girls, and the decision was taken out of their hands.

The twins ran ahead, clambered over the fence and were at the house before he could open the gate for Shauntelle.

He deliberately slowed his steps, unwilling to cut this time alone with her short.

"Thank you for being so patient with my daughters," Shauntelle said, slipping her hands into the pockets of her blue jeans. "I know they can be quite a handful, and I appreciate how you've dealt with them."

"I enjoy being around them," Noah said. "They're good girls."

"So have you been out riding much while you were here?" Shauntelle asked as they walked toward the house.

"Not really. I'm not so crazy about horses."

"Are you kidding? What kind of rancher are you?" She was smiling at him now, and he knew she was teasing him.

"The kind of rancher who spent too much time getting bucked off them as I was helping my father train them." Noah tried not to sound bitter, but he couldn't help the tone of his voice.

"So your father trained his own horses?"

"He did, though most of the horses my father had trained have been sold already. The ones we used today were older horses that my mother got from one of her brothers. But like I said, they're great horses. I wouldn't put your girls on them otherwise." Again he heard a defensive note drifting into his voice.

"I know you're careful," Shauntelle said. Her words of affirmation warmed him more than he thought they should. "I've seen you working," she continued, "and I've heard you talking to the employees at the arena. I know safety is important to you."

He didn't bother to respond to that. But there was something else he felt he needed to deal with.

He slowed his steps, turning to her. "I don't know how to say this without sounding awkward, but about yesterday—"

She stopped and turned to him. "Please don't apologize. It wasn't only you."

Her comment made his heart skip its next beat. And once again he was lost in her eyes. Once again he wanted to kiss her.

And then his hand was on her shoulder, his fingers gently caressing her neck. To his surprise, she didn't look away. Instead she reached up and covered his hand with her own, her eyes still holding his.

He wasn't sure what would've happened next. He didn't have a chance to find out.

"Are you guys coming?" Millie was hanging out the door. Her voice echoed across the yard, bouncing off the trees and shattering the silence.

"Guess we've been summoned," Noah said, disappointed at how shaky his voice sounded.

"Good way to put it," Shauntelle said, but she didn't turn away either. Which raised questions and launched an undercurrent of feelings. He wanted to touch her, to connect with her, while his head fought with his lonely heart.

Her hand lifted, and for a moment he thought she would touch him, but all she did was tuck her hair behind her ear, smile at him, then turn away.

They walked to the house together, but they didn't move very quickly; it was as if neither of them were in any rush to rejoin responsibilities and family.

"So, you're baking for my cousin's wedding on Friday?" Noah asked, trying to find a neutral topic of conversation.

"Ella called last night in a panic. She has a caterer for the supper who couldn't do desserts. Then her dessert caterer bailed on her."

"Will you have time?"

Shauntelle lifted one shoulder in a vague shrug. "It's an excellent opportunity to showcase my own upcoming business. And I'd like to help Ella out."

Her comments made sense. But it also meant she would be at the wedding. And he doubted she would take her daughters. The thought created possibilities.

Be careful. You're not staying.

But even as he formulated that thought, he looked around, heard the birds singing in the willows along the edge of the dugout. Above him, the sun shone down from a sky that seemed unnaturally blue.

He felt a settling in his soul in the quiet. Regardless of the bad memories, the ranch still appealed to a deeper part of him. Then he looked over at Shauntelle, and that same soul felt a deeper yearning.

She was watching him, a puzzling expression on her face.

"Do you miss this?" she asked, as if she could read his thoughts.

He didn't want to delve into why she was asking. Mere curiosity, probably. But the kiss they shared seemed to color every interaction they had.

"I miss the space. The quiet." That much he dared to admit.

"Your mother said your life here wasn't easy."

Noah shoved his hands in his pockets, once again struggling with the negative emotions and memories being on the ranch also created. "I'm surprised she admitted as much."

"I got a sense she didn't always know what to do. How to help you."

Noah stopped, as his feelings battled with his mother's current reality. She was alone, living on a ranch that was falling apart, waiting and hoping he would return.

"I'm sure that's true." He caught her frustrated look and sensed that his curt answer annoyed her.

"Now that I'm a mother, I know how many decisions need to be made every day," she said. "I think every mother alive feels like she hasn't done enough. I know I sure do. I feel bad that my daughters are growing up without a father, and I feel bad that we have to live with my parents. That I don't have a house to give them."

"But did you ever struggle with the decisions you had to make as a wife or mother?"

She stopped, laying one hand on the railing of the stairs as she turned to him.

"It was always a struggle. Roger was gone a lot, and I know he was accomplishing a great deal. He was a doctor, for goodness' sake. But I often thought he could have done more for us. That I should've advocated more for the girls and me. I should have made him realize his choices hurt his family."

She wasn't looking at him, but Noah heard the anguish in her voice.

"But he was a good man doing good work."

Shauntelle tapped her fingers on the wooden railing, as if delving into the past. As she did, he compared himself to her husband. The man whom everyone admired. The man her parents saw as a hero. And then there was him. The man who everyone thought was responsible for her brother's death.

"I knew what he did was important," Shauntelle said. "But I understand what it's like to live with a dominant personality. It's hard to put yourself forward. It was a mistake I think of often. Had I been more demanding, had I pushed for what I wanted and what the girls needed, I might not be living in my parents' house trying to figure out how to support my daughters."

Noah was surprised to hear the sorrow in her voice and the anguish twisting her features. He was about to say something when she pulled her hand back and turned away from him. "I'm sorry. I've said too much."

She jogged up the steps and went into the house. Noah stayed behind a moment, her words ringing in his ears. What she'd told him wasn't the picture of domestic stability he'd imagined her life to be. And even though it had cost her much, he also couldn't help feeling relieved. The hero that her parents admired wasn't everything he was cracked up to be. It felt small to be happy about that, but it also reassured him, for some reason.

Monday morning. The doors were coming today.

Shauntelle had tried to call the door installers all weekend but could not get in touch. Now it was time. She didn't want to go to the arena but had promised them she would meet them there.

Don't think about it. Don't panic. Look at the page you have to do right now.

She clenched her hands around the steering wheel, praying as she drove, for patience and for wisdom, wishing she could just get a break.

She knew she was being small-minded. She had gone through bigger things than this and come to the other side. But she was so tired of managing and turning and spinning and dashing, trying to make everything come together.

You can do this. Just be strong.

She pulled up to the arena, but in spite of her pep talk she couldn't stop the panic bubbling up when she saw the truck emblazoned with the name of the window and door company parked at the back entrance. They were already here. Her heart sank at the inevitability of her situation.

One thing at a time, she told herself.

As she opened the door of the arena, the familiar whine of saws and the pounding of hammers greeted her. Every day she came, something new was finished. It was encouraging, and she knew the members of the rodeo group would be very happy with the progress.

As she walked across the floor, she looked out for Noah but couldn't see him. She hadn't seen him in church yesterday, though his mother was there. Shauntelle didn't have a chance to talk to her either, because Fay left before the service was finished. Cord and Ella had walked out as well, so Shauntelle suspected they had brought her. As for Noah's absence, she was surprised at the disappointment she had felt. She couldn't help wondering if he stayed away because of her parents, or because church didn't mean much to him.

Not that it mattered to her.

And who are you fooling?

She put her hands on the bar of the door leading to the foyer and hesitated. The moment she had been dreading was here. She sent up another prayer, pushed the door open and stepped inside. The first thing she heard was laughter, then the beeping of a Bobcat backing up.

Then shock surged through her. There, directly in

front of her, was a large, beautiful opening on one side of the support, with one gorgeous door already installed.

When? How?

Then she saw Noah partway down the foyer, hands on his hips, sawdust sprinkled on his shoulders as he talked with an unfamiliar man. He looked up, then walked over to her, his expression enigmatic.

"What's going on? How did this happen? When did this happen?" Shauntelle hardly knew which question to ask first. She gestured to the doors, then looked back at Noah. "I don't understand."

"What's to understand? The opening is in and the doors are being installed. Like you wanted." He sounded gruff, but a smile teased one corner of his mouth.

"I can see that. But there was no opening on Friday." She looked over at the installers consulting with Kyle. "How did this happen? And when?"

"I talked a few guys into coming in over the weekend." He shrugged. "I don't usually work on Sunday, but I knew you were under the gun."

"That's why you didn't attend church yesterday."

He seemed to brighten at that. "Were you looking for me?"

She would not blush, but the more she tried not to, the warmer her cheeks grew.

"The girls were," she offered, knowing it was a lame excuse.

His smile created a peculiar trembling in her heart. This man was edging into her very being, and she thought of him too much. But he had just done a wonderful thing for her, and her relief erased restraint. So, instead of simply smiling her thanks and politely telling him how much she appreciated his help, she threw her arms around him and gave him a tight hug.

He seemed stunned, but only for a split second. His arms came around her and he held her close. And for one blissful moment, as she laid her head against his chest and clung to him, appreciating his strength and his nearness, she didn't care who saw and what they thought.

Her world shifted on its axis in more ways than one. She wouldn't have to go talk to her supervisor at the bank and grovel for more money. Her plans could carry on, and she didn't have to pay the deliverymen extra.

And Noah Cosgrove was hugging her.

"You are an answer to prayer," Shauntelle said, pulling away from him.

His surprised look almost made her laugh. Then he grinned back at her, and as her eyes held his, she once again felt that connection that sparked between them every time they were together.

"Noah, when you're done flirting can you come over here and help me?" Kyle called out.

Noah took a step away from her, but his eyes still held hers. Before he left, he gave her a secretive smile.

Shauntelle watched him leave, then turned her attention to the installation of the doors she hadn't thought would happen until tomorrow, and felt—for the first time in a while—things turning around.

Shauntelle watched the progress as long as she dared, chatted with one of the installers, answered a couple of questions, then left for her job in the bank.

The afternoon seemed to crawl by, however. She wanted to head to the arena and see how work was progressing on her dream. And maybe chat with Noah. It wouldn't hurt for her to thank him again.

"Hey, Shauntelle, do you have a minute?" Courtney

Waters stopped in, then glanced down at the notepad on Shauntelle's desk. "What's this?"

For the second time that day, Shauntelle blushed as she looked down. Various iterations of the letter *N* stared back at her. She hadn't even realized she had doodled them. She ripped the paper off the pad, balled it up and tossed it into the garbage can.

"Whatcha doing?" Courtney asked.

"Nothing," she said, trying to sound casual and not self-conscious. "Trying to come up with…trying to… I need a logo for my restaurant."

"With the letter *N* in it?"

"And what are you hanging around to tell me?" Shauntelle folded her arms on her desk, deflecting Courtney's question.

"Do you have time to see Mrs. Cosgrove?" she asked with a curious glint in her eye. "Mother of someone whose name happens to start with, say, the letter *N*?"

I'm not blushing, Shauntelle thought. Instead she held Courtney's eyes, and her chin lifted, then she nodded. "I sure do," she said, hoping she sounded confident and in charge.

"Noah seems like an awesome guy," Courtney said, a dimple flashing in her cheek as she grinned back at Shauntelle, clearly jumping to her own conclusions. "In fact, if I wasn't married…"

"Let's not keep Mrs. Cosgrove waiting, shall we?"

"Let's not," Courtney said, and then flounced off, leaving the door open.

Mrs. Cosgrove was still using her crutches as she came into Shauntelle's office, but her cheeks were pink and her eyes bright, and she was smiling.

"I hope you don't mind me seeing you on such last-minute notice," Mrs. Cosgrove said as Courtney escorted her into her office.

"Not at all," Shauntelle said, walking past her. Ignoring Courtney's knowing grin, she closed the door, then pulled out a chair. "Have a seat, Mrs. Cosgrove."

"Please call me Fay," Mrs. Cosgrove said as she settled into the chair, looking around her office. "This is a nice office. Though every time I think of you, I imagine you at the Farmer's Market."

"I only work here part-time," Shauntelle said, settling in behind her desk.

"Seems that you have a lot of part-time jobs. That must keep you busy—and now you're thinking of starting a restaurant."

"I'm hoping that will become my full-time job," Shauntelle said, folding her hands on her desk. "So what can I do for you, Mrs. Cosgrove—I mean, Fay?" she added when Mrs. Cosgrove put up a warning hand.

"My friend had brought me to town to have a look at the arena," Fay said. "It's coming along really well. I'm excited about the courtyard."

"Thanks for that affirmation," Shauntelle said. "I know that will be a nice addition. Especially because it looks out over the park."

"It will be lovely. But enough chitchat. I came to see you because I was in town and wanted to invite you and your daughters to dinner on Wednesday evening."

Dinner. That was not what she'd expected.

"I don't want to put you out," Shauntelle hedged, not sure how to say no as her feelings battled with her practical side. Part of her wanted nothing more than to spend an evening with Noah and his mother in their beautiful, peaceful house. But the cautious part of her cried danger.

Though she knew things were changing between her and Noah, the reality of their futures always hovered over the relationship. She had her daughters to think of, and her own future to plan. Noah also had his own goals, and she knew they didn't include staying in Cedar Ridge. It would be foolish to get involved with him. Spending more time at his ranch with his mother...

"You won't be putting me out at all," Fay said, breaking into her thoughts. "I was going to get Sepp Muraski from the Brand and Grill to put together supper for us. Noah was going to take it home."

So Noah was in on the plans. She wondered how he felt about it.

"I still don't feel right about this." But when she saw Mrs. Cosgrove's wide smile, Shauntelle knew she had made a mistake. She made it sound like she was accepting.

"I'm so excited that you're coming. I know Millie said she would enjoy it."

And how did Mrs. Cosgrove know Millie would enjoy it? Had they been talking to each other?

"Of course she would," Shauntelle said. Her daughter seemed to think the sun rose and set on the Cosgroves, which had caused tension between her and her parents.

"That's perfect then," Fay continued. "I'll go talk to Sepp and make arrangements."

It looked like that was it. Shauntelle had no more space to refuse. However, there was no way she was allowing Mrs. Cosgrove to do any of the preparations.

"No. Please don't talk to Sepp. If we are coming for dinner, then allow me to cook it," Shauntelle said, standing up as if to make her point even more clear.

To her surprise, Fay didn't object at all. "That would

be fantastic. You're such a good baker and cook. I'm not saying no to that."

Shauntelle just gave her a tight smile. Though she felt a teeny bit manipulated, she couldn't say she was unhappy with the situation.

She just wondered what Noah would think.

"Where are the girls?" her mother asked as she put the plates on the table in the kitchen of their home. She and her father had just come home from work, and he was on the phone with a supplier putting an order in.

"In their room," Shauntelle said as she cut up the lettuce for the salad. Chili simmered in the slow cooker and the buns were buttered. Supper was almost ready. "They said they had homework." Though Shauntelle doubted they were busy with that. She rather suspected they were making their own plans. When she had told them about Mrs. Cosgrove's invitation on the drive home, they didn't seem surprised. They were clearly in on the scheme.

"I'll call them now," her mother said.

Soon they all sat around the table. Her father said grace, and Shauntelle started serving.

"So what are you going to do about the doors for the restaurant?" her father asked as she handed him a plate. "I have to say I'm upset that Noah didn't plan better for that."

"You don't need to be," Shauntelle said, setting the casserole dish on the table. "The doors are all installed. And everything went perfectly."

Her father shot her a shocked look. "How did that happen? This morning you were worried that you'd have to pay those installers extra. No thanks to Noah."

Shauntelle held her father's gaze, tired of his fault-finding. "It happened because Noah worked over the weekend to make sure everything was ready for my doors when they came this morning. And it wasn't his fault. It was mine."

Her father's only reaction was to narrow his eyes and then look away. Shauntelle fought down a beat of frustration and sat down. She wanted to challenge her father's attitude, but felt at a disadvantage. She was their daughter, but she was also a guest in their home.

Then she felt her mother's firm touch on her arm and turned to see her shake her head, her eyes wide with warning. *Don't talk about it.*

She hadn't intended to, but she was tired of how both her parents seemed determined to be so unforgiving. She understood their loss. She had lost her brother and was grieving too. To be stuck in this angry stage of grief wasn't healthy.

"I think we need to move past this," she said, unable to keep her comments to herself anymore. "Noah was proven innocent."

"How can you say that?" her father said, his voice hard. Angry. "He knows he's guilty. Otherwise why would he—" He stopped there, his lips clamped together.

"Why would he what?" Shauntelle asked, wondering what in the world her father referred to.

"We don't want to talk about it," her mother said, the anger in her voice letting Shauntelle know the subject was off-limits.

Supper was a tense and quiet affair. When it was over, Shauntelle told her parents she and the girls would do the dishes.

By the time everything was cleaned up, it was time to put her daughters to bed. They complained, but Shauntelle ushered them down the hall to their bedroom, ignoring their pleas for just a few more minutes. She wanted them down for the night so she could retreat to her own space. The tension in the house was exhausting.

When they were settled in the bed they shared, she sat down on the end, her hands folded in her lap as she looked from one girl to the other, knowing she had another sticky issue to deal with.

"Are we in trouble?" Millie asked, as usual very attuned to her mother's moods.

"Did you do something you should be in trouble for?" Shauntelle countered, wondering what they would come up with.

Millie and Margaret exchanged hurried glances, and Shauntelle guessed they knew she wanted to discuss Mrs. Cosgrove's invitation.

"We just wanted to see the horses again," Margaret said, the words bursting out of her.

"Margaret," Millie cried out, slapping her hands in frustration on the bed. "What are you doing? It was a secret."

"What secret?" Shauntelle asked, determined not to let their antics make her smile.

Another quick exchange of glances.

"Millie?" Shauntelle pressed, guessing her most outspoken daughter was the true instigator.

Millie sighed, trying to look defiant but failing. "So I maybe, might have phoned Mrs. Cosgrove," she said, avoiding Shauntelle's gaze, tilting her head to one side as if considering what to say. "And perhaps, maybe, I possibly said that we wanted to come visit her again?" Her voice rose up on that last line, her hands turning over in a gesture of confusion, as if unsure herself how this all might have come about.

Don't laugh.

"And the other thing," Margaret said, nudging her sister.

"What other thing?" Shauntelle asked her other daughter.

Now it was Margaret's turn to avoid her gaze as she twisted her hair around her finger.

"Margaret?" Shauntelle pressed. Millie was vibrating with tension, but Shauntelle kept her eyes on Margaret, knowing if anyone would cave, it would be her.

"We just wanted a daddy," Margaret finally wailed, looking distressed. "We miss our dad, and we love you, but Mrs. Cosgrove said Noah would make a good dad. And we think so too."

Shauntelle could only stare at the girls, her mind scrambling to catch up to their plans.

"We know you're lonely," Millie put in. "And it's a lot of work to take care of us all by yourself. And we are tired of living in Gramma and Grandpa's house. Mrs. Cosgrove said there's lots of room in hers. And then we could all live on the ranch together and ride horses every day. We really like Mr. Noah."

"Did Mrs. Cosgrove say this, or did you come up with the idea?" She felt she needed to verify a few things before she called Noah's mother.

"Are we going to move?" Millie, ever the optimist, pounced on the tiniest little opening and tore it open.

"No." Shauntelle said the word with extra force. "We aren't talking about that. At all. I just want to know who said what."

Millie looked over at Margaret, who bit her lip as if unsure what to tell her. Shauntelle kept her own expression hard, determined to sort this out.

"I talked to her," Margaret said finally. "And… and…"

She hesitated, and Shauntelle could see Millie was about to put her two cents in but she held up her hand, shot her a warning look and turned back to Margaret, who was still twisting her hair around her finger.

"And," Shauntelle prompted.

"And she said we could come over whenever we wanted. And that she was lonely in her big house and that it had a lot of room."

"But I thought she meant we could move in." Millie made one last plea. "I really thought that's what she said, and Margaret and I were talking about how fun it would be to be cowgirls. And to have a dad…" Her voice faltered and trailed off as she started crying.

Margaret put her arms around her sister and joined her.

Shauntelle scooted closer, pulling them both against her, shaking her head at their plans and dreams.

"Oh my dear girls," was all she could say, holding them close and kissing the tops of their heads.

"Are you mad at us?" Millie sniffed, her head tucked against Shauntelle, one arm around her waist.

"A little bit," she said.

Margaret sighed. "I don't want you to be mad at us. We just…we just wanted you to be happy. Because you haven't been very happy since we moved here."

"That's because your uncle Josiah died, and because your daddy died, and Gramma and Grandpa are sad."

"Do you miss Daddy?" Millie asked, pulling back to look at her.

Shauntelle knew she was expected to say yes. Of course she missed Roger. Yet, as she looked into her daughter's earnest gaze, she found herself not thinking of Roger, but of Noah.

So she simply nodded.

"We used to miss him," Margaret put in. "But not so much anymore."

Shauntelle laid her head against Margaret's, releasing a confused sigh. What was she supposed to say to that when she felt the same? Shouldn't she still be grieving? In the grief group she had gone to, some widows and widowers were still struggling even after four years. And here she was, two years later, feeling ready to move on.

What kind of wife was she? But even more, what did it say about her relationship with Roger?

"It's okay if you want to get married again," Millie put in. "We won't be like some of those spoiled kids on TV shows who don't want their mommy to get married again. We don't mind. Especially if it's Noah."

And just like that, her confusion morphed into frustration. "I wish you wouldn't keep talking about him," she said, trying to keep her tone light.

"But we like him," Millie said, batting her eyes. "And we think you like him too."

Shauntelle couldn't deny that. Because hovering behind her wavering emotions was the reality that she was attracted to him. In spite of who he was and how her parents felt about him.

"So does that mean we can go over to Mrs. Cosgrove's house?" Margaret asked, sensing her weakness.

"You let me talk to her first," Shauntelle said. "I'm not making any promises." She gave them each a stern look to bring the point home.

They nodded, looking solemn, which Shauntelle knew meant the point was taken.

"Let's say your prayers, and then you both need to get to sleep."

A few minutes later they were tucked in, kissed and Shauntelle was closing the door on their bedroom. She stayed there a moment, making sure they settled. She heard her parents talking and was about to go across the hall to her room to call Fay when she heard her name mentioned.

"… Shauntelle lets the girls spend too much time at the Cosgroves'."

Her mother sounded upset, which wasn't a surprise. Ever since Noah Cosgrove had come back to Cedar Ridge, her mother had become more unhappy and morose.

"I could take them out on a hike. I haven't been able to do that for a while, but now that we've got Nick working for us I could. It would be fun," her father was saying.

"And it would give them something else to talk about besides the Cosgroves. Honestly, each time I hear them mention that man's name…"

Time to go.

Shauntelle stepped into her bedroom and closed the door behind her. She was thankful her father wanted to spend time with her daughters. He had done little of that since they moved here.

However, her parents' ongoing antagonism toward Noah was creating a perplexity of emotions.

Because she knew, even though her mind shouted out a warning, that thoughts of him were slowly invading her heart and soul.

Chapter Nine

"I'm so thankful you made supper for us." Noah's mother looked from him to Shauntelle then to the two girls, who were scooping the melting ice cream out of their bowls. "Wasn't it delicious, Noah?"

"Beyond delicious." Noah glanced over at Shauntelle, surprised at how happy he was to see her in his own home. He had seen little of her lately, and he thought she was avoiding him. Then his mother told him she was coming for supper.

"So now, I think we should go for a walk." His mother was already getting up as she spoke.

"Are you sure?" Noah asked.

"Oh, don't you fuss over me." His mother flapped her hand at him. "I've been feeling good lately."

"I can see that for myself," Noah said. "I'm so glad."

The past few days, in spite of her broken leg, his mother had smiled more, her eyes had sparkled more, and she seemed to be brimming with enthusiasm. Though he guessed much of it had to do with him being on the ranch, he also suspected part of her increased vigor was because of Shauntelle's daughters.

His mother hadn't come right out and said as much,

but Noah was sure that she and those adorable twin girls had put this whole supper scheme together. And right now, with Shauntelle sitting across from him, he didn't mind one bit.

"Why don't you go out for a walk, and I'll take care of cleaning up," Shauntelle said as she stood as well.

"Not a chance, my dear," his mother said. "When you make the supper, you shouldn't have to do the dishes. Noah and I will do them once you leave."

Shauntelle looked like she was about to object again, but Margaret was already pulling her away from the table. Noah thought maybe he should stay behind, but then Millie grabbed his hand.

"You have to come too," she said, tugging on his hand, giving him no choice but to follow.

He gave in and they all trooped out the door behind his mother, who was moving surprisingly fast for someone on crutches. She was down the stairs of the porch before he could offer to help.

"I thought the girls would like to see the barn, and then we could go look at our cows," his mother said, heading down a path leading to the back pasture where the cows were.

"How many do you have?" Shauntelle asked, trying to keep up with her.

"About thirty," his mother said, stumping along as if she was a woman on a mission. "Noah keeps telling me I should get rid of them, but I like having them around. Them and the horses. You know my husband and Noah trained those horses."

Most of the horses he and his father had trained together were gone. The only ones left were the ones she got from Uncle Boyce. But he didn't want to make his mother feel bad. So he chose not to correct her. Instead he followed his mother, the girls easily keeping up with her as she told them about the ranch, explaining where it came from and the history.

Noah held back, guilt slithering once again into his soul. He knew the ranch had been passed down through three generations of Cosgroves and that he had always been expected to carry on the tradition. But that would have meant working with his father.

"I feel I should explain about how we ended up here for supper," Shauntelle said, pulling him back from the dark place he'd been going to. She lowered her voice, slowing her steps to stay out of earshot of his mother and the girls, who had now disappeared around the side of the barn they were walking toward.

Noah raised his hand to stop her, feeling the faintest twinge of disappointment over her need to clarify. "I think I know what happened," he said, also speaking quietly, also slowing his steps. "I overheard my mother talking to one of your daughters a few days ago. It sounded like they were planning something."

"I'm sorry. Those girls are, for lack of a better word, incorrigible."

"So is my mother."

They both shared a smile, a lingering gaze. Her daughters and his mother were well ahead of them, but he was in no hurry to catch up.

"The supper was delicious, and I want to thank you for bringing it," he said, not sure what else to say. He felt like he was back in high school, trying to make conversation with a girl he liked and find a polite way to ask her out.

Of course, this wasn't what was happening here.

"I think—"

"I wonder—"

They spoke at the same time and laughed, tried to start again, and then quit.

"You first," he said.

She looked away, biting her lip. "This is embarrassing for me, but I need to bring it up."

She paused again, her hands shoved in the back pockets of her blue jeans. He felt a flicker of concern at her serious expression and her hesitation. He wondered if what she needed to bring up had anything to do with her brother.

So he waited, trying not to get too nervous. He had enjoyed supper tonight. Enjoyed having Shauntelle and her daughters join them. Their laughter and good humor brought joy to a house that had had little joy in it for many years.

He hoped she wasn't telling him they couldn't come anymore.

And why does that matter? You're leaving.

But somehow it was getting harder to be so emphatic about that as he'd once been. And the woman beside him had much to do with that shifting emotion.

"So, what do you need to bring up?" he prompted, her long pause making him nervous.

"It's my daughters." She sighed, then shook her head. "You may as well know they have taken something your mother said and run with it." Another pause, another sigh. "It was a simple comment your mother made," she finally said, "about the size of your house and how there was lots of room. Millie and Margaret…well… they seemed to think that was an invitation from your mother—"

She stopped there, and once again he was intrigued to see a flush rising up her neck, coloring her cheeks.

"An invitation for what?"

She sighed again, then turned to him, looking embarrassed. "My daughters seemed to think your mother was asking them to live with her. And me, I guess." She rolled her eyes at that. "As if that's not bad enough, they have been talking about you…and…well…me."

You and me.

Seemed kind of nice to think about. But he needed to clarify.

"You and me…" he encouraged.

Another sigh. Another flush as she flapped her hand between them. "Us. Together. They were saying silly things like how you could be a…" She shook her head. "This is genuinely embarrassing, but I'm scared they're telling you or your mother anyway. But they seem to think you would make a good dad and that you and I could be together."

"Me. A dad." The thought tantalized and teased. He and Shauntelle and her incorrigible daughters.

"The girls have vivid imaginations and can weave an entire story out of a few words. I'm so sorry, but I figured you should know." She hurried her steps, as if she wanted to get away from him.

He caught her by the arm, halting her forward momentum. "Hey, don't worry about it. I've been around your girls enough by now to know how they act. And what they're capable of."

The relief on her face made him smile. "They are quite something. But I felt I needed to tell you. I didn't want them tossing it at you out of the blue."

"That would certainly have caught me unawares." But as he noticed her grateful expression, his mind tested the idea. He and Shauntelle, with her little girls. A family. For a moment he allowed himself to imagine all of them here on the ranch.

He tilted his head to one side, as if studying Shauntelle from another angle. He reached up and gently tucked a strand of hair behind her ear, just for an excuse to touch her. His breath caught in his chest, and once again it seemed as if time wheeled to a standstill.

He wanted to kiss her.

"Are you guys coming? It's so awesome here!" Millie called out.

Noah pulled back, looking around to see where her voice was coming from. And then he saw her, crouched on her hands and knees, looking out the open door of the second-story loft of the barn. Margaret stood behind her, clearly unwilling to take the risk Millie was.

"I'd really like it if you moved back," Noah said, stifling a beat of fear and striding toward the barn, his eyes locked on Millie.

"It's perfectly safe up here," Millie called out, grinning down at him.

"I still think you should back up," Noah said, getting closer. The way she looked over the edge gave him the creeps. The last thing he wanted or needed was for something to happen to Shauntelle's daughters on his ranch.

"Millie, please listen to Noah," Shauntelle added. "It's not safe where you are."

"I'm okay, Mom."

"I want you to move now." Noah couldn't help the hard tone of his voice, but she had to know he wasn't kidding. "And come down from that loft please."

Millie held his gaze as if challenging him, but then, thankfully, she crept back from the opening.

Relief flooded him, and he hurried into the barn, to make sure the girls came down. His mother was at the bottom of the ladder, looking up.

When she saw Noah, she clapped her hand to her chest, as if she too had been afraid of what might happen.

"I'm so glad you're here. I tried to tell them not to go up until you came, but Millie was determined to have a look."

"I'm not surprised," he said, then clambered up the ladder just as the girls came to the opening.

Instead of looking contrite, Millie had a mischievous expression on her face.

"Were you scared something would happen to us?" she asked, rocking back and forth on her feet.

"Yes I was," Noah said, wondering how she could act so blasé after being reprimanded. Once again he felt sorry for Shauntelle, having to deal with this little spitfire.

"I was being careful," Millie said confidently.

"You were way too close to the edge," Margaret put in. She sounded upset. And Noah didn't blame her—he felt the same.

"I'm glad you listened anyway," Noah said. "Now let's get you down here, where it's safer."

"I saw you with my mom." Millie changed the subject with an alacrity that almost made Noah smile in spite of what had just happened. "She sure is pretty, isn't she?"

Noah was glad that Shauntelle had given him a heads-up as to where her daughter's thoughts were heading.

"I want to see you go down," was all he said.

"I thought you would kiss her," Millie continued, not the least put out by his orders.

If he was the blushing sort, Noah was sure his face would have been beet red.

Instead he pointed to the ladder. "Down. Now." He made his voice extra firm, extra hard, trying not to let what that little stinker said get to him.

Thankfully they both clambered down, joining his mother and Shauntelle at the bottom.

His mother looked penitent. "It was my idea to show them the barn, and I did tell them not to go up to the loft." Then she looked over at the girls, frowning. "But I wish you would have listened to me."

To Noah's surprise, both girls looked down at the ground, now contrite. Millie dug the toe of her runner into the loose dirt, making a hole, and Margaret twisted her hands around each other. His mother created a sense of shame in them that he couldn't.

"What do you girls say to Mrs. Cosgrove and Noah?" Shauntelle prompted.

They both mumbled an apology, and then his mother ruffled their hair. All was forgiven, and Millie shot out the door, off to the next adventure.

"Millie, you need to stay with us!" Noah called out.

Thankfully Millie stopped in her tracks and trudged back to join them.

"Thank you for listening," Noah said.

"You sound just like a dad," she said with a pout.

"I think he would be a good dad," Margaret put in, sounding demure.

Noah glanced at Shauntelle. She was blushing again and avoiding his gaze. He couldn't blame her, not after what she had told him.

"Don't you think Mr. Noah is a good dad?" Margaret asked Shauntelle.

"What else did you want to show the girls, Mother?" Noah asked, cutting off any other embarrassing thing either of them might say.

His mother gave him a sly smile, but Noah didn't bite. "I thought you had something else you wanted them to see," he pressed, giving her a warning glance.

"Right. One of the farm cats had kittens. I thought that would be fun for Millie and Margaret," his mother said, seeming to take the hint. "They're in the feed shed beside the corrals."

"Kittens? You have kittens?" Margaret looked enraptured. "I would love a kitten. Can we have one? Please?" She turned to her mother, pleading.

"We'll just look at them," Shauntelle said with a rueful smile. "You know we can't have a cat at Gramma and Grandpa's place."

Margaret's frown showed Noah what she thought of that. "Gramma and Grandpa's house is no fun. I wish we could live here."

Noah couldn't stop a quick glance at Shauntelle, who was looking upward as if petitioning God for patience.

"Let's be thankful that Mr. Noah and Mrs. Cosgrove let us come and visit," Shauntelle said, turning back to the girls.

Very diplomatic.

"Let's go look at the kittens." His mother headed out the door.

Thankfully, this time the girls stayed with them as Noah and Shauntelle followed. Though he had warned them to do exactly what they were doing, a small part of Noah wished they would hurry ahead so he could snatch a few more moments alone with Shauntelle.

He glanced sidelong at her and he wondered, from the smile teasing a corner of her mouth as she held his gaze, if she thought the same.

* * *

"All we need to do is paint the walls, and we'll be ready for the kitchen equipment next week." Kyle waved his hand as if to demonstrate.

Shauntelle stood with her hands on her hips, looking at the transformed space. Yesterday she hadn't been able to come here, which had created a mixture of disappointment and relief. She could still feel the heat of mortification she experienced when Margaret told Noah he would be a good father.

Since their visit to the ranch on Wednesday, she hadn't seen Noah at all, and wondered if he was avoiding her. Yesterday he was gone for a meeting with the rodeo group when she came to the arena, and she hadn't seen him yet today.

She tried not to let his absence matter, but deep in her heart, it did.

"This looks amazing," Shauntelle said, studying the walls separating the kitchen area from the dining space. They were all dry-walled and taped, transforming the large room into so many possibilities. She could see where the tables and chairs would go, what the kitchen would look like. All the dreams she had spun now stood in front of her, solid and real.

"Noah was hoping he could be here to show you this," Kyle said. For a moment Shauntelle wondered if he could read her thoughts.

"It's okay. I know he's busy," she said, hoping she sounded more casual than she felt. His words had ignited a tiny spark of hope.

"I don't think he's ever too busy for you." Kyle gave her a knowing wink, and Shauntelle wondered if her feelings for Noah were that obvious.

"Well, I'm sure he has many other important things

to do." Shauntelle gave Kyle a forced smile, then looked once more around the space that would soon be a full-fledged restaurant. Anticipation rose, battling the usual nerves.

Would this work? Would she get enough customers? Could she make enough to support herself and her daughters?

"Anyway, I thought I would stop in and see how things are going. See if you needed anything."

Kyle shook his head. "We got this. You just make sure the equipment comes next week, and I think we'll be in good shape."

She gave him a quick nod, then hurried back to her parents' home to finish making the bowls of trifle she had planned on serving at the wedding.

Her parents were at work but had told her they had an appointment in Calgary that evening. All very mysterious, and Shauntelle didn't have the mental energy to figure out what that was all about. So she arranged for her friend Tabitha to pick up the girls from school and keep them overnight. Millie and Margaret were thrilled, though they had casually suggested they could maybe stay at Mrs. Cosgrove's place instead.

Shauntelle hadn't even acknowledged the bait they floated past her.

Two hours later, she smoothed the last layer of whipping cream on the trifle, sprinkled some chocolate swirls on it and set it in the carrier. She arched her back to ease the kink out of it, then hurried to her bedroom to change.

She knew she wasn't required to dress fancy. But she would be setting the desserts out in front of the wedding guests and wanted to look professional.

And you want to look your best for Noah.

She tried to ignore the taunting voice as she got dressed. She wore black dress pants and a soft pink, sleeveless lacy top that flowed past her hips. She curled her hair and clipped the sides up with some sparkly barrettes, letting the curly tendrils frame her face.

Eye shadow, eyeliner, mascara. Then a touch of lipstick.

She stood back and gave herself a critical look in the mirror, wondering what Noah would think. Then she packed up the food and drove to the hall, unable to keep down anticipation at the thought of seeing him again.

Shauntelle wove her way through the many cars and trucks in the parking lot of the hall and backed up to the door leading to the kitchen.

The kitchen was empty. Though the blended scents of supper still lingered, the counters were spotless and empty. Ella had wanted Shauntelle to come well after supper was over, and it looked like the caterer had cleaned up and left already, so she had the place to herself.

The door from the kitchen to the hall was closed, but Shauntelle could hear laughter, music and the happy chatter of wedding guests.

She found a shim to hold the outside door open for her, then brought the boxes and containers from the car into the kitchen.

On her fifth and final trip, the door to the hall burst open just as she stepped into the kitchen. Ella bustled in, her cheeks pink and her smile as bright as her sparkling eyes. Her hair was pulled back and held in place with flowers. Her dress had an ivory lace bodice and flowing gauzy material that fell to the floor in a cloud. She looked as ethereal and beautiful as any bride could.

"Oh I'm so glad you're here," she cried out, her hands

pressed to her stomach. "I'm absolutely starving. What did you bring me?"

Shauntelle didn't have a chance to answer. Ella was already flipping open the lid of a pastry beside her on the counter. She filched a lemon tart out and started eating it, her eyes closed with an expression of bliss.

"Oh, this is amazing," she murmured, licking her fingers. She took another one, but before she ate it she shot a guilty look over her shoulder. "Sorry. I'm just so hungry. I couldn't eat supper because I was so nervous."

Shauntelle grinned as she set up one of the two cupcake stands she'd brought. "You help yourself. I think it's important that you approve of the merchandise before your guests do."

"I like how you think," Ella said. She polished off the lemon tart in two more bites, then opened another box and pulled out a cupcake. She turned it in her hands, admiring the tiny sugar roses. "This looks too good to eat, but that won't stop me." She took a bite and sighed again, looking back over her shoulder. "Seriously. You should go into business with this." Then she giggled. "Wait. You are. Noah said the restaurant is looking great. I'm so excited you're doing it, and so is everyone I know. It's high time we had a decent restaurant in town."

And why did the mention of Noah's name give her more of a thrill than knowing people were excited about her new business?

"I'm glad to hear that. I'm nervous about it all," she said, opening another box of cupcakes and arranging them on one of the cupcake stands she had brought.

Ella took another bite and licked her lips. She held up the remains of the cupcake she was eating. "If your cooking is half as good as your baking, it will be fantastic."

"It certainly will."

The deep voice coming from behind her sent shivers dancing down Shauntelle's spine.

She turned, and there he was. His long, dark hair tamed and combed down. White shirt cinched by a blue tie. Dark blue suit setting off his broad shoulders, narrow waist. He looked taller and, if anything, even more handsome.

She couldn't seem to keep her eyes off him.

"You look nice," he said, slipping his hands in his pockets, tilting her a crooked grin.

"Thanks." Why did the sight of him take her breath away? Why did his smile make her heart forget what to do?

"I think I'll just leave you two alone," Ella said, waving her half-eaten cupcake at them.

"No, it's okay—"

"It's fine—"

Noah and Shauntelle spoke at once, then both stopped, and Ella's smile widened.

"I should join my guests," Ella said, grabbing her dress with one hand while still holding the cupcake. "Just bring the food out when it works for you."

Noah held the door open, and with a rustle of satin and tulle, Ella left.

The door fell shut behind her, closing off the chatter and noise from the hall.

"If I'd known you were here, I could have given you a hand hauling all this stuff in."

"It's fine. I managed."

"You always seem to manage," he said, a curious tone in his voice. "Very independent."

"I've learned that the hard way."

He held her gaze a moment as if he wanted to ask her more, then looked around at the boxes and plastic containers that held the cake stands, platters and cupcake towers. "I think I can figure this out. Can't be any harder than installing glass doors."

They shared a quick glance and a smile, and her heartbeat shifted again.

"Besides, I could use a break from talking about the arena and my plans with all the relatives," he said, opening a box beside her. "So I guess these go on this platter?"

She sensed he wasn't leaving, which was fine with her. So she gave him directions, telling him what went where.

Soon they had all the cupcakes arranged, and the cakes and pies and fruit platters set out.

"I guess we may as well bring this out."

As they did, people stopped what they were doing and drifted over to the tables.

"Wow. That stuff looks amazing."

"I've never seen anything so beautiful."

"There goes the diet."

Shauntelle felt the lift of pride at the positive comments and admiring looks. She resisted the urge to fiddle with the food arrangements.

"I see the desserts are coming out," a voice boomed from the sound system. "I think we should let the bride and groom have first dibs, and then everyone else can help themselves."

Before Shauntelle had the last platter of fruit on the table, Cord, Ella, and Cord's children, Susie, Paul and Oliver, were already taking plates and filling them up.

"This seriously is incredible," Ella said, catching

Shauntelle's hand as she passed her. "I'm so glad the other girl ditched me. I don't think I would've gotten anything half as nice as this."

Shauntelle could only smile. The compliments from the wedding guests gave her a badly needed boost of confidence.

She couldn't help a quick glance Noah's way, only to see him grinning at her.

Right about now, if someone were to ask her, she would say life was pretty good.

Chapter Ten

"**Y**our mother seems to be doing fairly well," Reuben was saying as he picked the cake crumbs off his empty plate.

"In spite of having a broken leg, she is." Noah flashed his cousin a smile, but he had a hard time concentrating. The whole time Reuben talked, his attention was on Shauntelle, who had been replenishing the dessert table and fussing with the arrangements. Her eyes were bright and her cheeks flushed, and she looked amazing.

The lights had been turned low, and the dance had already begun, but people were still helping themselves to the desserts.

"So Cord is sure happy," Reuben said.

"Yeah. He is," Noah replied, dragging his attention from Shauntelle and back to his cousin. "I'm happy for him. He's had a difficult time. And I'm happy for you and Leanne too. It seems that all my cousins are finding their way through life. Making a home here."

Shauntelle was cleaning up the plates and bringing them into the kitchen. She looked like she was getting ready to leave.

"You even listening to me?" Reuben was asking.

Noah blinked, then gave his cousin a rueful smile. "Sorry. A bit distracted."

Reuben looked over to the table where Shauntelle was now tidying up in earnest. "Well, I can see why. She's beautiful."

Noah didn't need to add anything to that.

"I hope you're asking her to dance before she leaves," Reuben said, setting the plate aside.

Noah had been thinking the same thing, but somehow, to do that in front of his family seemed to create a commitment he wasn't sure he was ready for.

"I don't know."

"What's not to know? She's single. So are you. She's here. So are you."

"It's not that simple," he returned, looking back at his cousin. "And I think you understand exactly what I'm talking about."

"Her parents? Her brother?"

Noah sighed, tugging the knot of his tie loose. He had abandoned the jacket half an hour ago.

"That's part of it, but I think she's getting past it," Noah said. He knew she was still grieving her brother, but what she had told him about Josiah being a risk taker gave him some hope for closure, at least with her.

"So what's the other part?" Reuben asked.

The music had grown louder and quicker, and Noah saw his mother holding court with Carmen Fisher, Cord and Ella. She was chatting away, underlining a point with a wave of her hand, eyes bright and looking happier than she had in ages.

"Staying here." Noah turned. "My mother would love nothing more than if I took over the ranch, but I don't think I can."

"I understand. I went through the same thing," Reuben said, his expression growing serious. "You and I both know what it's like to live with a difficult father."

Noah shoved his hand through his hair, trying to align his past with his present. "I can't help it," he said. "Every time I'm on the ranch, I remember how brutally hard I worked. Dad was always pushing, always demanding. I really don't have many good memories there."

Reuben scratched the side of his face with his forefinger, as if thinking. "My father pushed me hard too. Lots of difficult times. Except I had a chance to make peace with George. I won't deny that it's been difficult, but I've forgiven him, and I know that my son, Austin, gives him great joy. We're working through it, and I'm really glad. I can't imagine being anywhere but Cedar Ridge right now."

His words fell into Noah's mind like rocks tossed into a pool, disturbing a surface Noah had struggled all his life to keep quiet and calm.

"I know you have some bad memories of the ranch," Reuben said, putting a hand on his shoulder. "But you can make new ones. And much as you've been talking about leaving, I also know it gets harder for you to leave your mom behind."

"The guilt is real," Noah said, adding a laugh, trying to bring some levity to the conversation.

"Being with Leanne, making our own wedding plans, has created a richness in my life I didn't know was missing. I think the same could happen with you and Shauntelle."

Noah glanced over to where Leanne and Shauntelle were talking.

Before he could stop him, Reuben grabbed him by the arm and dragged him over to the women.

"I think it's time for us to have a dance," Reuben said to Leanne. "And Noah, why don't you dance with the lovely Shauntelle?"

Reuben pulled Leanne into his arms and spun her away, leaving both of them behind staring at each other.

This was a slightly awkward moment, but Noah knew he had to capitalize on it. So he held his hand out to Shauntelle. "Can I have this dance?"

"I haven't danced in years," she said with a little shrug.

"That makes two of us," Noah said with a grin. "But I'm pretty sure you'll catch on."

Her chuckle was all the encouragement he needed. He slipped one hand around her waist and caught her other hand in his. They made a few fumbling steps, then just as Noah had promised, they found the rhythm and soon were two-stepping across the dance floor in perfect sync.

Shauntelle was laughing, and he took a chance and spun her around. She missed the next step and lost her balance, and he caught her.

"Maybe a little too ambitious," he said.

"You never get anywhere if you don't take any risks," Shauntelle returned, grinning.

They caught their rhythm again, but no sooner was he ready to give her another twirl than the music shifted down. The lights were lowered, and a plaintive country music song came up. Violins gave cues, and the singer's voice became a quiet, hushed crooning as she sang of memories and making new ones. Just as Reuben had said.

For a moment, Noah wondered if Reuben had made a specific request, the lyrics were so apt. He looked at

Shauntelle, shrugged, and then, taking advantage of the moment, pulled her close and slowed his steps.

She followed his lead, and to his surprise and joy, she tucked herself against him, her head on his shoulder. Noah laid his head on hers, closing his eyes, letting the music take them along. Enjoying this moment with this beautiful woman in his arms. They didn't speak, both seemingly unwilling to break this magical moment. This felt right. It felt good, and Noah didn't want the song to end.

As they turned around on the dance floor in each other's arms, possibilities danced on the edges of his thoughts. He and Shauntelle and the girls. On the ranch, just as they had dreamed of.

Could he do it? Could he, as Reuben had suggested, make new memories?

The song wound to a close, and when it ended, Noah stayed where he was, still holding Shauntelle, tucked in this moment of possibilities.

He drew back, looked down at Shauntelle and gave in to his impulse.

And right in front of his cousins, his mother and assorted members of the Cedar Ridge community, he kissed her.

Shauntelle couldn't believe he had done that. When he pulled away she immediately wanted to kiss him again, but reason intervened, even as her heart beat like a mad thing.

Had that really happened? Had Noah Cosgrove just kissed her in front of all these wedding guests?

"I should… I should go," she said, unable to look away from the dark intensity of his deep brown eyes. "I have to clean up. Go home. Clean up the leftovers. Tidy up." Her words spilled out like her daughters' beads out of a box. Unorganized and random. Just like her thoughts and emotions.

But even as she explained why she had to leave, even as he nodded as if agreeing with her, her hand stayed on his shoulder and his on her waist.

"Do you need help?" he asked, his voice hoarse.

She shook her head but sensed that he would help her anyway.

The music started up again. A polka this time.

"This would be our cue to leave," Noah said, a smile curving his lips.

Shauntelle pulled away, ignoring the knowing looks people gave them, and headed into the kitchen.

She had been washing plates as they emptied so she had little to do. She was disappointed that Noah hadn't followed her, but as she put the last of the cupcakes away, the door of the kitchen opened and he entered carrying a stack of empty plates, a half-eaten cake balanced on the top one.

"Not much left of all this," he said, setting it down.

"You don't need to help. You should spend time with your family."

"I'm sure I shouldn't," he said as he rolled up his sleeves and dumped the platters into the sink of soapy water. "Especially not after that little display."

But his smile showed her he hadn't minded the "display" at all.

"I should let you know your darling daughters called my mother before we left for the wedding," he said as he washed the dishes. "They invited themselves over for tomorrow. I somehow doubt you know anything about it."

"I don't, and I apologize for my daughters' boldness." Shauntelle felt a tremor of embarrassment, but the grin on Noah's face told her he didn't mind the girls' forwardness.

"Don't apologize. I'm looking forward to it," he said, rinsing off the platter. "So where do you want the clean dishes to go?"

And just like that, he shifted the conversation to a more comfortable place. It didn't take long to finish cleaning up, and when they were done, he helped her pack everything into her car.

The sun had set and the air was cooler. Shauntelle shivered as she closed the hatch of the car, then turned to Noah. He was right there, looming over her, tall, strong. And he smelled so good. Her heart twisted at the thought that he might kiss her again.

"Thanks again for all your help," she said, wishing she didn't sound so breathless. "And I guess we'll see you tomorrow."

"Looking forward to it." His eyes gleamed in the gathering dusk, and then he ducked his head, brushed his lips over hers again. Just like she hoped he would. "Text me when you get home," he said, his voice warming her soul.

She felt a surprising urge to cry.

Text me when you get home.

How long had it been since anyone was looking out for her like that? Since someone cared to know she made it home? Even when Roger was alive, she had to rely on herself.

"I will," she said. She gave him a wavering smile, then got into her car. And as she drove away from the hall, in her rearview mirror she saw him standing in the parking lot, watching her leave.

And her heart sang.

The drive back seemed to take mere seconds. Her

mind replayed that dance, that slow movement in his arms. The kiss. The other kiss. As she let herself in the house, she was so thankful her parents were gone and that the girls were staying overnight. She knew she had a sappy look on her face, and she was humming.

She banished second thoughts for now. She wasn't looking into the future. For now her heart was full, her soul quiet.

For now, she only wanted to think as far as tomorrow. When she and her daughters would spend time with Noah and his mother. At the ranch the girls thought would make the perfect home.

The picture lingered, and she pushed it aside. One page at a time, she told herself.

Don't look too far ahead.

The pernicious voice intervened, and though she wanted to dismiss it, she knew she had to be careful. Cautious. She had her daughters to think of, and she wasn't in any position to indulge in whims. Not when Noah was still talking of leaving.

Chapter Eleven

"I'm so glad Gramma and Grandpa are gone for the weekend," Millie said as she cuddled the kitten.

"Why do you say that?" Shauntelle asked, settling herself down beside Margaret, who was also holding a kitten on her lap, stroking its head with her forefinger.

"They wouldn't be happy that we're here," Millie said, rubbing her nose on the kitten's.

Shauntelle couldn't help a quick look Noah's way, disconcerted to see the frown on his face. It was still something she struggled with, the disconnect between her parents' anger toward Noah and her own growing attraction.

She knew her parents were stuck in their lack of forgiveness, and she also knew she had to address it. Regardless of what happened between her and Noah.

Noah crouched down in front of Millie, who was stroking another kitten. "You know you guys can come here anytime to see the kittens."

"But will you be here all the time?" Trust Millie to cut straight to the chase.

It was a question that had taunted Shauntelle the past couple days.

Yesterday after church, they had come to the ranch and had lunch with Noah and his mother. And then Noah had taken the girls out on the horses again. It had been a wonderful day, and what made it even nicer was the fact that Shauntelle and the girls had come back to an empty house. They didn't have to deal with the repercussions of their visit.

When Shauntelle had asked what was keeping her parents so busy over the weekend, they had given her some vague answers about visiting old friends and taking time off from the steady work of the gas station.

While Shauntelle was happy for them and Nick had been only too willing to take over for the weekend, she was still curious about what was going on. They seemed secretive. And she didn't like it. Currently she had enough other questions in her life.

All seemed to center on the man sitting with her daughters. Could she continue to be involved with Noah if he was still thinking about leaving?

The mother cat came to join them, batting a paw at the kitten on Margaret's lap.

"I think the mother is getting nervous," Noah said. "Maybe we should put the kittens back and let her take care of them."

The girls didn't even protest, which surprised her. Noah could get them to listen and obey him far easier than she could.

Moments later the kittens were safely tucked away and the mother was purring. "I think she's happier now," Margaret said, taking a moment to run her finger over one of the kitten's heads again. Then she turned to Noah. "Can we go pet the horses?"

Noah glanced over at Shauntelle, and she gave him a quick nod. "But only for a few minutes," Shauntelle warned the girls as they ran out of the barn. She wanted to be home when her parents came back.

She stood, brushing the straw off her pants, thankful for this quiet moment with Noah.

He gently plucked a piece of straw out of her hair, and then let his fingers linger on her cheek as he smiled down at her.

"I'm glad you came today," he said. "It's been so nice having you and the girls here."

Shauntelle looked up at him, questions hovering. Did she dare ask? Did she dare think she had any right?

But she had responsibilities. And she needed to know.

"I need to talk to you," she said, not knowing how else to broach the topic.

"That works out well," Noah said. "I need to talk to you too."

She held his gaze a moment. "We both know things are changing between us. I think you know I'm attracted to you…" She let the sentence trail off, feeling self-conscious.

"I kinda got that feeling." Noah chuckled as he rested his hand on her shoulder and tightened his grip. "And that works out great, because I'm attracted to you too."

She smiled, and taking a chance, took his hand in hers, stroking over his rough knuckles while looking down at the faint scar on his thumb. "I don't know how else to say this so I may as well just come right out. I have my girls to think about, and my own future to take into consideration. In my previous marriage I spent a lot of time working around my husband's plans." She stopped there, a surprising hitch in her voice.

"You must still miss him," Noah said. Was that a faint note of disappointment in his voice?

"I miss having someone to share life with." Then she looked up into Noah's eyes, holding his gaze. "He's the father of my daughters. But recently I don't miss him like I used to."

Noah's smile gave her hope.

"But like I said, I spent a lot of time working around what he wanted. I…I…can't do that anymore. I have my own dreams and plans, and I'd like to see them come to fruition."

Noah's smile slipped, and he released a light laugh. "You and most of Cedar Ridge. After you left the wedding, all I heard was people saying how excited they were for you to open your restaurant. I told them it wasn't just pastries you excelled at."

"Thanks for the endorsement."

"I'm excited for you to open your restaurant too. And I'm excited to see the arena getting finished. It will be a good thing for the community."

"The community is important to you, isn't it?" she asked.

"My relatives are here. Cedar Ridge holds a lot of memories."

Her mind slipped back to what Fay Cosgrove had told her. "Your mother said some of your memories of this ranch aren't so pleasant."

Noah's eyes seemed to drift over the yard, then back to her. "They aren't. This barn, the corrals, the whole ranch in fact—every part of it has an unpleasant memory of my father. My mother has tried to make me see his point of view, but it's been difficult. My grandfather let this ranch run into the ground, and my father was working his hardest to fix it. To get it back to where it was before. I sometimes think he was competing with my mother's family. Or at least showing he was as good as any Walsh could be."

"That's a hard burden to carry. And that's not a fair burden to put on you," Shauntelle said, her voice quiet.

"It wasn't, and like I said, it made for some bad memories." He stopped there, but looked like he wanted to say more.

"Are you guys coming?" Millie stood in the doorway of the barn, one hand on the doorjamb and the other on her hip, looking like a put-out debutante.

"Yes we are coming," he said, pulling his hand away as if to retreat.

As Shauntelle followed him, she felt a mixture of hope and apprehension.

Did she dare believe her and Noah could make a go of this?

"That was a nice visit," his mother said as Noah cleaned up the dishes.

"It really was. I enjoy having Shauntelle and the girls here." He knew it was stronger than that, but he also knew enough about his mother not to give her too much to run with. He was still trying to balance how he felt around Shauntelle with figuring out what future he could create for them.

He didn't want his mother to know the direction of his thoughts while he still sorted them out.

But one thing was sure—having them here pushed some of the older memories down. Created new ones that made him smile. That made him wonder if he could stay in Cedar Ridge and make a life on this ranch. As much as his father had built bad memories, there was still a large part of his heart that yearned for the open spaces and life on the ranch.

"I enjoy having them around too." His mother finished the last of her tea, then set the cup on the table. "It's as if this house, and this ranch, have gotten a new lease on life with them here." His mother ran her finger over the handle of her mug, looking contemplative. "I know living here hasn't been easy for you. And I haven't been the mother I should have. I see how Shauntelle is with her girls, how careful she is with them and how much she protects them. I should've been that kind of mother." She looked up at Noah, her eyes full of pain. "I hope you can forgive me for not standing up for you."

Noah saw the sorrow on her face, then walked over, bent down and gave her a tight hug. "You are always a good mother," he said. "I'm thankful now and I was thankful then for everything you've done for me. You are an example of faithful love, and of faith." He brushed a kiss over her head, then straightened.

The words she spoke released the remnants of anger and frustration he had felt about her. Was it time to move on? Make new memories here? Did he dare believe his feelings for Shauntelle could overcome the pain of the past?

"Thank you for that," his mother said. "That helps me a lot. But I'm also hoping that you can find redemption here. I see how you are with Shauntelle and those girls, and I know I'm being forward here, but I'm getting older and I can't afford to be tactful. I know you could be a good father to those girls, and I know you can be a good husband to Shauntelle."

"I'm not so sure about the good husband part," Noah said, thinking about Shauntelle's husband. "Kinda hard to go up against the hero that her previous husband was."

His mother folded her arms over her chest, her eyes

narrowed. "I've had chances to talk to those little girls. I don't believe he was unkind, but I think he was often absent, following his own dreams. So to me he's not such a hero."

Noah had to smile at the defensive tone in his mother's voice. However, what she said also gave him hope.

"That may well be, but he was still their father. And I wouldn't want to disrupt their memories." As he spoke, he realized where his thoughts were going. As if it was a foregone conclusion he would be a part of Millie's and Margaret's lives.

And, more importantly, Shauntelle's.

The gleam in his mother's face showed that she was headed in the same direction too.

Then his phone buzzed in his pocket, and he pulled it out, glancing at the screen.

He frowned a moment, trying to figure out who was texting him. Then he realized it was the owner of the company he was planning to buy. How could he have forgotten about that?

Because it doesn't truly interest you? Because you've been distracted by a pair of hazel eyes, and a pair of adorable girls?

Could it be that's not where your heart is?

Been trying to call, the text said. We need to arrange this sale before you leave on your trip.

"I've got to call this person," he said to his mother, puzzled by how Gord Tkachuk had gotten hold of his cell number.

"Is that the man with that construction company you're thinking of buying?"

"How did you know?"

"He's called here a few times."

Noah frowned at her. "I don't remember you mentioning it."

"I forgot. Besides, I thought he would call you on your cell phone."

Now he realized why Gord hadn't stayed in touch. "I didn't give him my cell phone number. He must have gotten it from my old partner." The man who had bought Noah out after Josiah's death.

"So what are you going to do?" his mother asked.

He paused, still not sure what to think or what plans he dared make. "I'm not sure."

His mother held his gaze, her expression serious. "You must be sure," she said. "For your sake and for Shauntelle's."

Noah knew she was right. Knew he had to be careful. Being with Shauntelle would be an all-or-nothing proposal.

Did he dare change his life for her?

Chapter Twelve

"Hey there, how are things going at the arena? Kyle not ragging on the employees too much?"

Shauntelle pressed her cell phone to her ear, to cancel out the sounds of drills on the other side of the arena's wall. She had been taking pictures of the walls of the restaurant so she could order prints and decorations when her phone rang.

When he had called her on Monday night to tell her that he had to go to Vancouver for a quick trip, she was struck by a combination of emotions.

One was the fact that he felt he had to tell her he was leaving. As if she had a right to know.

The other was that he hadn't told her why.

"It's going well," she said, moving into the kitchen area of the restaurant, to get farther away from the noise coming from the arena. "The guys are putting in the seats. That's the drilling you hear in the background. The lights are up, and the fellow installing the scoreboard is here with his crew."

"And the restaurant?"

"All painted and ready for the next step." It was hard to keep the excitement out of her voice. "The chairs and tables are arriving in a week. I still can't believe it's all coming together. I'm standing in the kitchen now, and it's like a dream come true. I'm reluctant to cook in it and make it all dirty."

"After the first pot boils over, it will all be fine," he said with a light chuckle that dived into her soul.

"I'm sure."

"Sounds like things are under control. I thought I would let you know I'll be back late tonight." He paused and she waited, her heart beating with anticipation. She so wanted to ask him what he was doing in Vancouver. When he'd first come, she heard rumors he would be buying a new company there. But she didn't know if they were at that place yet, so she kept silent.

"That's good."

"I was also wondering if it would be possible to go out tomorrow evening. Just the two of us. If it works for you."

Out. A date. He was asking her out on a date. Would he do that if he were leaving? Would he lead her on like that?

"What time?" she asked, wishing she didn't sound so breathless.

"I was hoping to take you some place in Calgary, so would it be possible to pick you up after work? I know you're done at three o'clock."

Her mind felt scrambled as she tried to figure out how this would work. She could ask her mother to pick up the girls from school and watch them. Now that her father had a full-time worker at the garage, her parents had more free time.

And what would happen if her father found out she was getting them to babysit so she could go out with

Noah? For a moment the complications of her situation clouded her anticipation of spending time with him.

"I'd have to figure something out," she said, clasping one arm around her middle, fighting down her hesitation and second thoughts. "Find someone to watch the girls."

His pause told her he knew enough not to suggest her parents.

"But I'd love to go out with you," she added, just in case he thought she was looking for an excuse to say no.

"I'm glad we agree on that." He released a light laugh that, to her ears, sounded relieved. "I'll call you once I'm back. We can make further plans."

"Sounds good." She waited, wondering what else to say, then realized he was waiting for her to hang up. "Are we going to do the 'you hang up, no you hang up' thing so popular with teens?" she teased.

"We could. Never really played that game."

She chuckled. "Oh, how much you have to learn, grasshopper."

"I know." Another pause. "I'm looking forward to tomorrow. A lot."

"Me too."

"So, you hang up," he said.

And just for fun, she did.

Noah looked at himself critically in the mirror, then ran his fingers through his hair to make it look more natural.

He hadn't been this nervous in a long time. Which was ridiculous, because he and Shauntelle had been together plenty of times recently, but this was an actual date, which could mean a large step toward something more permanent.

His visit to Vancouver had been enlightening. Walking around the downtown streets, along the seawall and through Stanley Park, places he had always dreamed of being, wasn't as much fun on his own.

The whole time he was there, all he thought about was open fields, horses, two spunky girls and one beautiful woman.

His mother was in her easy chair, reading a book. She looked up when she saw him come into the living room and grinned at him.

"You're looking very spiffy, and quite happy, I might add." She set her book down.

"And you're looking rather smug, I might also add," he said with a grin.

"I'm just pleased for you," she said.

Apprehension shivered down his spine. He wanted to stop her, tamp down her hopes. And in the process, his own. He hardly dared believe that his life had come to a good place.

"One step at a time," he told his mother.

"I know you have to be careful, but don't be too careful. Sometimes you have to latch on to things when they come your way." She held out her arms, and he bent over and gave her a hug. "You're a good son. You've always been a good son. I wished I could've been a better mother."

Noah caught her hands and gave them a squeeze as he pulled away. "You've had your own things to deal with. You've always been a loving mother to me. And I'm so thankful for you in my life. God has blessed me. And I know it."

He was surprised to see a glimmer of tears in her eyes. And in that moment of vulnerability, that moment between mother and son, he felt a rush of love for her stronger than any he'd felt before.

Something important had shifted between them. And he knew he would do whatever he could to make her happy.

His phone dinged, and he glanced at it and smiled. Rows and rows of heart emojis filled the screen.

Then his phone dinged again. It was a text from Shauntelle apologizing for the previous text. The girls had gotten ahold of her phone.

He laughed and replied to her text with a smiley face.

"You better get going," his mother said. "Girls don't like to be kept waiting for dates."

Noah bent over and brushed a quick kiss over her soft cheek, then left, whistling.

As he walked over to his truck, he heard the sound of a vehicle coming around the corner and up the driveway. He frowned, wondering whom it could be. He didn't think his mother was expecting any company, or else she would've told him.

A compact car, rusted and dented, pulled up beside him, and an older man got out.

"Are you Noah Cosgrove?" he asked, striding over with purpose.

"Yes I am," Noah said, puzzled as to whom this might be.

The stranger handed him an official-looking envelope, and instinctively Noah took it.

"This is a citation, and the rest of the package will explain in more detail," the man was saying. "You have thirty days to answer the complaint with the summons. If you do not show at court, you'll get a default judgment against you."

"Are you serving the legal papers?" Icy fingers

clutched his heart as the man nodded. "Who is this from?" Noah asked.

"Not allowed to discuss that. All I can tell you is they are court papers and there is a time limit." Then he walked back to his car.

Noah ripped open the envelope, and with shaking fingers pulled out the legal documents.

And as he scanned them, trying to understand the legalese, he realized what the papers meant.

The Rodriguez family was suing him.

Chapter Thirteen

"Why isn't Mr. Noah coming?" Millie sat on the bed, her hands resting on her knees. "And you're all dressed up so pretty."

Shauntelle's heart felt like a rock in her chest. She wasn't sure where to put her emotions. Just a few moments ago she'd gotten a text from him saying he had to cancel their date to go to Vancouver.

But what sent a chill blooming in her chest was the last thing he wrote.

I think we should give each other some space.

The words were like a physical blow. The line was so cliché, she was disappointed that he used it. If he was breaking her heart, surely he could come up with something more original.

Why had he strung her along like this? Why even bother if this was going to be the endgame?

Something wasn't adding up, but she felt too distraught to delve into it.

"Are you crying?" Margaret asked.

Shauntelle gave her a tight smile, shaking her head. "No, I think I got something in my eye."

"That happens to me sometimes," Margaret said

sympathetically. "You just have to blink a bunch of times and it will go away."

If only it were that easy.

She tucked the girls in and gave them a perfunctory kiss. Now she needed to get out of the house, away from her mother's questions and her daughters' concerns.

She closed the door behind her and leaned against it a moment, the tears that Margaret had noticed now drifting down her face. She swiped at them, angry that she'd allowed them to fall. Angry that Noah had created this disappointment in her. Angry that once again she had put herself in a position to be let down by a man.

She strode down the hall into the kitchen and grabbed her car keys off the hook.

"Do you mind if I go out for a little while?" she asked her mother. "I need to go for a drive."

Her mother looked up from the crossword puzzle she was working on. "Are you seeing…Noah?"

Her hesitation as she spoke his name was like a fitting counterpoint to the entire situation. Her parents didn't like Noah. Never did. Never would.

Maybe it was just as well.

"No. I'm not."

"Is everything okay?"

No. Nothing was okay. Everything was all wrong.

"I just want to get out." And before her mother could ask her any more questions, she walked out to the car, got in and drove. She had no plan; she simply needed to get away.

She drove to the arena. Nobody was working there, and the doors were locked. But she walked around the back, where the courtyard of the restaurant was taking shape. Noah had promised her it would be ready by opening day.

Noah and his promises.

The thought choked her.

She didn't know why she was torturing herself, but she pulled her phone out again and once more read what Noah had sent her.

I think we should give each other some space.

Some space.

It was a classic breakup text. Why couldn't he just come out and say it? Why was he hiding behind these superficial comments?

And why wasn't he man enough to phone her?

She wanted to toss the phone across the field. As if that would do any good.

She leaned against the wall, sliding down until she reached a sitting position. She wrapped her arms around her knees and laid her head on them, and in spite of her decision to keep her heart whole, the tears drifted down her cheeks and a sob stuck in her chest. It annoyed her that Noah had brought her to this. She had cried enough tears these last few years, but those tears were for a reason. They were for a loss.

This was a loss as well, but deep and harsh disappointment was woven through it.

Dear Lord, she prayed, *why did You bring him into my life only to pull him out again? Why did You put me through all this? It would've been so much easier if I had simply followed my instincts and not let him into my and my daughters' lives.*

Her daughters. What was she going to tell them? They thought Noah was amazing. Thought he was some kind of hero who would rescue them and bring them to a new life.

Her anger took over the tears. She wished he had never come back to Cedar Ridge. Wished she'd never put herself in this position, with a vulnerable heart. Thinking she could count on him.

She took in a shuddering breath, knowing she had to pull herself together. She and her daughters had been on their own even before Roger died. This was nothing new to them; they could handle this again.

But even as she stood and wiped her eyes, her heart twisted in her chest. Because she knew forgetting Noah and putting him behind her would be harder than she ever realized possible.

Maybe even harder than when Roger died.

And behind that treacherous thought came another, almost as hard to face.

Maybe her parents were right about him. He wasn't the right person for her and her daughters. He wasn't a good man.

She wished she could shake that thought off, but like the anger and pain, it, too, clung.

You're on your own, she told herself as she looked at the courtyard of her restaurant and her future. *From here on it's just you and your Lord and your family and your kids*.

The next few days were a blur of busyness—working at the restaurant, the bank and getting ready for the Farmer's Market on the weekend. Thankfully Noah didn't come back to the arena. But every night, when Shauntelle was alone in her bedroom, sorrow took over. So she threw herself into her work and tried to be positive for her daughters.

And all the time Noah stayed away.

The girls were asking about him, but she put them off with vague answers. Once she was ready to talk about it more, she would let them know what a disappointment he had been.

By Friday she felt as if she might make it. Each day still brought the reminder of the loss of dreams, but she drew on the coping skills that had stood her in good stead after Josiah died. After Roger died. Her parents said nothing, though Shauntelle was sure they knew what was happening.

She was putting the finishing touches on a cake she had been baking when her mother came back from the gas station.

"Do you want a cup of tea?" she asked her mother when she came into the kitchen.

Her mother waved her offer off, then sat down at the table, heaving out a heavy sigh.

"You seem tired," Shauntelle said, concerned. In spite of her own troubles, Shauntelle had noticed that her mother had looked especially drawn and weary the past week.

"A little. Lots on my mind," she said, but her answer came out forced. Then she gave Shauntelle a gentle smile. "And how are you doing? I noticed that you haven't been at the Cosgrove ranch the past week. At all. Even the girls were grumbling about that."

Shauntelle looked back at the cake she was icing, wondering what to tell her mother and how. She would be happy, that much she was sure of, but it bothered her that she couldn't share this struggle with her.

"Is…is everything okay between you and Noah?" Her question came out quietly, almost hesitantly.

"Do you care?" The sharp tone in her voice surprised even Shauntelle. She didn't usually snap at her mother.

Then, to her surprise, she felt her mother's hand on her shoulder. "I care that you are hurting. I care that he's gone and that you've been so sad this week. I'm sure things will work out."

Shauntelle just shook her head. "I doubt it. I think it's over." She hadn't been in contact with Noah since that horrible text, and she had no desire to find out what was going on in his life.

"Maybe it's for the best," her mother said, patting her shoulder. "Given everything that has happened or might happen…" Her voice trailed off.

Shauntelle wondered what she was going to say, but didn't have the energy to ask.

"I should let you know your father wants to take the girls out tomorrow afternoon," her mother said. "Now that Nick is working more, he has time to do something with them."

Shauntelle nodded. "That sounds good. Where does he want to go?"

"He thought he might take them for a walk up Horseman Creek."

Shauntelle doubted her daughters would appreciate the walks her father liked to take, but she was thankful he was making the effort. "It's not supposed to be such nice weather tomorrow though," she added, glancing out the window. She'd been watching the forecast herself, guessing that the Farmer's Market would be moved indoors if it rained. Which was just as well. She'd heard, through the workers' coffee-time chatter, that Noah was returning on Saturday to do a quality control check.

So it would work well if she could be tucked away inside the old arena. It would keep her away from Noah and any potentially embarrassing and awkward meetings.

"He wanted to go in the morning and be back before the rain comes," her mother said.

"I like that. It would be good for them to spend some time together."

"I agree, and Shauntelle…about Noah…like I said, it's probably best…" Her mother's voice faded away, and Shauntelle looked back. "Once this messy business is all settled…"

"What do you mean, messy business?"

Her mother chewed her lip, hesitating.

Shauntelle put down the spatula she'd been using and walked over to her mother. "What are you talking about?"

Her mother looked over her shoulder, as if someone else might come into the room, then back at Shauntelle.

"It was Noah's own fault," her mother said finally. "He shouldn't have sent us that money."

Shauntelle felt like she had to shake her head to sort out what her mother was telling her.

"Money? What money?"

Her mother's eyes slid away, as if she didn't dare hold her gaze.

"Mother," Shauntelle warned.

"It started a month after Josiah died," her mother said, wringing her hands in anguish. "We got a check from Noah for two thousand dollars, and a letter telling us how sorry he was. He's been sending us money ever since."

"How come I've never heard of this before?" Shauntelle felt a clench of nervous anxiety. "And why did you take it?"

"He owed that to us," her mother cried out, finally looking at her.

"He was found to be innocent. He wasn't at fault for anything that happened." Shauntelle stared at her mother, unable to believe she still thought Noah had anything to do with Josiah's death.

This was getting to be too much.

Shauntelle thought of Josiah's pictures sitting on the windowsill. The pictures that had prompted her comment to Noah. She walked over, grabbed three of them and brought them back.

"You remember where these pictures were taken?" she asked, setting them in front of her mother, commenting on each one. "This one was when he went bungee jumping. In this one he went hang gliding, and this one is him rock climbing. You don't have one of him surfing or backcountry snowboarding, but he did those things too. All things that gave my brother a rush, as he liked to say. You know Josiah loved taking risks. I've watched Noah at work. He's a cautious man and very concerned about his workers' safety. If we put everything together, I think you and I both know it was probably Josiah's own fault he died."

Her mother's eyes widened as her gaze flew to hers. "How can you say that about your own brother?"

"I think you know I'm right," Shauntelle said. "You know how foolhardy Josiah could be."

"If Noah wasn't at fault, why was he sending us this money? The lawyer told us it looked like he was guilty."

"Lawyer? When were you talking to a lawyer, and what money are you talking about?"

Her mother looked away, fiddling with her wedding rings. A sure sign that she was nervous or uncertain about something.

"Mother, you have to tell me what's happening."

"It was your father's idea," her mother blurted. "I didn't like it at all, but I thought it would help us."

"What would help you?"

Her mother twisted her rings around her finger once more, then sighed, facing Shauntelle. "We are suing Noah for Josiah's death."

And suddenly, like tumblers falling into place, everything made sense. This was why Noah left; this was why he had pulled away from her.

She spun away from her mother, unable to articulate any comments. She grabbed a cake, dropped it in the cake box and slapped the lid shut. She added it to the other cakes already in a larger box.

"I'm heading out to market," she told her mother, her voice tight. "Let me know when Dad comes home with the girls. I need to talk to him."

"You won't tell him I said anything?" her mother asked.

Shauntelle couldn't even look at her. "I'm not promising you anything. I don't even know what to think anymore."

She lifted the box, reminded herself to be careful in spite of her anger. Then she brought it out to her car and set it inside, beside all the other buns, bread and pies she was bringing to the market.

She got into her car and, without a backward glance, left her parents' place.

But as she drove, the only thing that seemed to resonate in her mind was one question.

Did Noah think she was a part of all this?

Chapter Fourteen

"Thanks so much. I hope you enjoy." Shauntelle tied a ribbon around the cake box and handed it to her most recent customer.

"I'm excited about this," Cass Kollier said, tucking the box in her portable cart. "Tabitha brought some of your squares and cakes to the vet clinic, and I knew I had to try them for myself."

"I hope you enjoy."

"I will, but I can tell you one thing—I'm not bringing this to work with me."

Shauntelle kept her smile in place as Cass left, then pulled in a weary breath. With that sale, all her inventory was gone, so she was done for the day.

Thanks to the dreary weather, the market had moved into the old arena, which was a mixed blessing. It meant she didn't have to worry about running into Noah. She had seen his distinctive red pickup parked there this morning and had prayed she wouldn't see him, and so far she'd managed to avoid him.

With a tired sigh, she bent over to pick up the now-empty containers when someone called her name.

Shauntelle straightened, looking over her shoulder

as her mother ran toward her, clutching her cell phone. "Shauntelle, something's happened!" she shouted out, sounding frantic.

"What is it? What's wrong?" Her heart dropped like a rock at the fear on her mother's face.

"Your father. He just called. He's stranded with the girls on the other side of Horseman Creek."

"What? How?"

"The creek came up with all this rain. They went farther than he had planned, and now they're stuck."

Shauntelle yanked her own phone out of her pocket while her mother went on about the creek rising and how they were unable to cross.

She called her father, waiting, waiting, and then, finally, she got through.

"Dad. What happened? Where are you?" she asked, trying not to panic.

"Creek came up...can't get across...stuck..." His voice kept breaking up.

"Where are you now?"

"Don't know..."

"How far up the valley did you go?" Shauntelle gripped the phone, her hands like ice and her heart thundering in her chest, keeping time with the rain that had started up an hour ago.

She waited to hear something from her father, but all she heard was crackling. She repeated the question.

"...about a mile...walked up a trail...river...can't cross back..."

"Stay on the line, Dad," Shauntelle said, then lowered her phone. With trembling fingers she switched to an app her parents had recently installed on their phone and hers. It enabled them to find each other's location.

The app opened, and she tapped on her father's name.

At first all she saw was a square grid of lines and white, and then slowly, a picture appeared. And there it was. A pulsing circle giving her a vague idea of where her father might be. She took a screenshot of it, then zoomed out and took another just to be safe. It meant nothing to her. Hopefully someone else could decipher it.

She returned to her father, thankful to still hear the crackling.

"Stay where you are," she said slowly and clearly, hoping her father heard her. She repeated the phrase, waiting, but there was no reply. "I'll figure this out."

She turned to her mother, who was hovering behind her. "Let me use your phone," she said, handing her phone to her mother. "Don't hit any buttons," she said.

Shauntelle was about to dial 911 then stopped. The local police weren't equipped for this scenario. They would forward the call to Search and Rescue. By the time they were mobilized, it would be another hour. She looked out at the rain now coming down in buckets. How long would it take before her children could be rescued?

Noah would know where they are.

The thought rose up, but she stifled it with her own objections. Noah would have nothing to do with her now. Not after what her parents had just done.

It's not for you; it's for your children. Your daughters and your father need his help.

Pride had no place in this situation.

"I'm going over to the arena," Shauntelle said.

"Why?" her mother asked.

"Because Noah is there. And he'll know what to do."

"No. You need to call the police." Her mother's voice was shrill with panic, and she grabbed her arm.

"By the time I call the police, it will take too long to get everything in motion."

"But Noah—"

Shauntelle had had enough of her mother's critical attitude toward Noah. "Noah is the best person to help Dad get out of this predicament he got my daughters in." She knew her voice was rising with a mixture of anger and panic. Her mother's shocked expression underlined that. "I will get him and he will get the job done because that's the person he is. I don't want to hear another word against him, Mother."

Without looking to see if she was coming, Shauntelle strode out the door and into the rain toward the arena. Once inside, she waylaid the first worker she saw, asking where Noah was.

"He's up there," the young man said, backing away. Shauntelle realized she must look like a madwoman, but she didn't care.

Shauntelle glanced around, and then saw him. Her heart folded in her chest as she watched his tall figure bent over a table, discussing something with Kyle.

How could she face him? How could she dare ask him for help after what her parents had done?

Swallow your pride, she told herself. *It's not for you; it's for your daughters*.

He straightened as she ran up the stairs to the top level of the arena. She knew the moment he saw her, because his hands dropped on his hips, and he looked from her to her mother trailing behind her.

His mouth grew tight, and his eyes hard. It broke her heart to see how he retreated from her. But she didn't blame him one bit.

"I'm sorry to have to ask you this," she gasped as she reached him. "But I need your help."

"With what?"

Again, she pushed aside her doubts and her own concerns and plunged right in.

"My father took the twins on a hike up the Horseman Creek. It came up with all the rain, and now they're stranded on the other side."

"Did you call the police?"

"By the time they mobilize Search and Rescue, it might be too late." Desperation had entered her voice. "Horseman Creek runs through your ranch and I figured you would know better where my father is and how to help him, Millie and Margaret."

Noah held her gaze for a moment, then, to her relief, gave her a tight nod. "Okay. I can do that for your daughters."

The fine distinction created another quiver of guilt. She wanted to tell him she'd known nothing about the lawsuit. But now was not the time.

"I have a screenshot of their last location," she said, pulling out her phone.

Her fingers were shaking as she swiped through to the screenshot. Noah stood beside her, bent over her phone, and she caught a whiff of his aftershave and the ever-present smell of cut wood that always surrounded him. Her heart tumbled, and her breath caught in her throat. In spite of everything that was happening, she wanted to lean against him and let him hold her up.

But she had no right.

"I know exactly where they are," Noah said, creating a flurry of relief inside her.

"What are you going to do?" Shauntelle asked.

"I'm going to the ranch. I'll take a couple of horses to get them."

"Thank you so much," Shauntelle breathed, knowing those feeble words were not enough for what he was about to do. She had no right to expect any help from him. But now it wasn't about her and him. As he'd said, it was about her daughters.

He turned and jogged down the stairs. Shauntelle turned to her mother. "I need to go along with him. Can you find your own ride home?"

"Someone from the Farmer's Market will take me home, I'm sure."

"Okay. We'll stay in touch."

"You be careful," her mother said.

"Always," Shauntelle said. "Besides, I'll be with Noah. I'm sure I'll be safe."

She added a heavy emphasis to those words, as if to remind her mother where her allegiance lay. Then she ran to catch up to the man she trusted the most to take care of her daughters.

Shauntelle followed him all the way to the ranch. Did she plan on coming along on the rescue?

Noah parked his truck by the corrals and stepped out into the driving rain, squinting against it as Shauntelle pulled up beside him.

"What are you doing?" he asked.

"I'm coming with you."

"No. I won't be responsible for your safety."

"I need to come along," she repeated, raindrops sliding down her face. "Please."

He looked at her and, in spite of the circumstances, could still feel a thrill of appeal, a lingering yearning for her company. He had missed her with an ache that consumed him, and he hated it.

And now she stood in front of him, pleading.

While his practical side said no, it was her daughters

and father stranded out there. He had handled enough cows and horses to know the protectiveness of a mother. He couldn't imagine what she was dealing with, and knew being left behind would be more difficult for her than coming along.

He grabbed two bridles and handed them to her. "You take these, I'll get the saddles."

He caught the horses and tacked them up in record time. It was surprising how quickly the old movements came back. Buckle, tie, slip, tug and adjust the cinches. He had often done this under pressure, and in a hurry. But he also knew enough to double-check everything. Make sure the cinches were tight enough and the bridles buckled up properly. Everything solid and secure.

"I need you to mount up so I can adjust the stirrups," he said to Shauntelle, holding out his hand to her. He helped her up into the saddle, and in spite of the tension between them and the pressure of the situation, he couldn't stop the twist of his heart at her touch.

He turned his focus back to the stirrups, loosening the buckle and sliding it up, then he did the other side. "Check this out—make sure you can stand up in the stirrups, and that you can clear the saddle."

It all looked good.

"Now you need some gloves, a better slicker and a hat," he said. Then turned and strode to the house.

He saw his mother watching them through the kitchen window, and he hoped she wouldn't ask questions.

When he'd left for Vancouver the second time, all he told her was that things had changed and he wouldn't be home for a while. He hadn't had the heart to tell her he wasn't taking over the ranch anytime soon.

He stepped inside the entrance and pulled open the

door of a cupboard that held a variety of coats and hats. To his surprise, he found an older coat of his, one he'd worn when he was much younger. He couldn't believe his mother still had it. As he opened another cupboard, sure enough, his mother joined them.

"What are you doing? Surely you're not going out riding in this rain?" she asked.

"Shauntelle's daughters and her father are stranded across Horseman Creek, and we're rescuing them."

Noah handed Shauntelle a pair of gloves that would probably be too big for her, a hat that seemed to fit and then the coat. Without a word to him, or even a glance his way, she put everything on.

"But this is terrible weather," his mother cried out.

"And that's why we have to go help them," Noah said. "Everything will be fine, but can you please pray for us?"

"Of course, and always." His mother walked over and put her hand on Shauntelle's shoulder. "You be careful out there," she said. "But you can trust that Noah will take good care of you. Listen to what he tells you."

His mother's assurances gave him a tiny glow. Sure, it was his mother, but the affirmation still felt good.

"I've got my phone with me," Noah said. "But I don't know how good the reception will be down by the creek. So don't worry if you hear nothing for a while."

His mother nodded and stepped back.

He marched out the door and down the steps, Shauntelle behind him, their feet rattling the wood, and slogged through the mud to where the horses stood waiting.

He untied one horse, gave her the reins and she mounted up. But before he climbed on his horse, he looked up at her. "We'll get them. Don't worry about that. They're okay for now. We just have to cross that river."

She gave a tight nod, then he vaulted up in his saddle, grabbed the reins, gave his horse a nudge in his flank and trotted out.

They stayed on the road for a few kilometers, then ducked into a trail he and his father had cut years ago. He knew where he was going, heading for the widest and most shallow portion of the creek. Thankfully the rain had eased off and was now only a slight drizzle. But it still made for miserable riding. He wondered how Millie, Margaret and Shauntelle's father were faring. Noah hoped he knew enough to find shelter for them. He also hoped he hadn't moved too far from where they first tracked him. Noah checked his phone, but he had no bars. He had hoped that, should things not go well, he could still contact the police to mobilize Search and Rescue.

They followed the overgrown trail, and in spite of the low-hanging trees and encroaching willows, it was still easy to follow. From time to time he looked behind him to see how Shauntelle was doing. She had her head down, her hat pulled low, and all he saw of her was her lips pressed together.

He turned his attention back to the trail, keeping the horse to a slow but steady trot.

After what felt like aeons, they came to the creek and he realized why Shauntelle's father and the girls couldn't cross. The creek was twice as high as normal and rushing, in full flood, carrying logs and debris.

They rode farther upstream and thankfully, the place he wanted to cross was shallower and passable. Noah pulled his horse up, waiting for Shauntelle to catch up. He turned to her, pulling his coat tighter around himself.

"This is where you stay behind," he said, his voice firm. In charge.

"No."

It was a single word, but spoken with implacable force. Noah guessed from the determined look on her face that even if he were to insist, she would follow him anyway.

He looked from her to the creek, now swollen to twice its depth. He had to find a safe way to do this.

Would her parents file another lawsuit if something went wrong?

He waited a moment, planning his trip.

"Just make sure you let the horse choose its own path," he warned her. "He'll know what to do." Then he turned, clucked to his horse and started across the creek.

Shauntelle fought down a beat of panic, wondering if she should follow. But her horse was already stepping into the creek.

One step. Then another. Shauntelle kept her eyes fixed on Noah ahead of her as he made his way. The water was now up to the stirrups of his saddle.

Please, Lord, keep us safe, she prayed, pleading as she clung to the saddle horn. She wasn't leading the horse at all now, just hanging on.

Step-by-step they worked their way through the surging water. Now and again Shauntelle felt her horse lose its footing, but quickly recover. Each time her heart leaped into her throat.

Noah glanced back a couple of times and gave her a tight nod of encouragement.

Then, finally, the water seemed shallower, and they were closer to the opposite bank. A few more steps and the horses plunged through the last of the water and up the soggy side and into the trees.

Noah stopped, looking back as Shauntelle came up beside him.

"You okay?" he asked, his hat pulled low, moisture dripping down his face.

She nodded, giving him a tight smile.

"It will be narrow through the next bit. I'm taking a shortcut to the trail your father was heading down. Just follow me."

"Of course" was all she could say.

"We'll find them," he said with an encouraging look. "We've gotten through the worst part. You did good."

He clucked to his horse, and again the horses picked their way around and over fallen trees. But at least they were on dry ground.

As she rode, Shauntelle gazed through the falling rain, trying to see, straining to hear anything from her father or daughters. But all she heard was the sound of the rain pattering on the leaves and the gentle plod of the horses' hooves on the wet ground.

After what seemed like hours, they came to a clearing. Noah stopped and pulled his cell phone out of his coat pocket, probably checking the picture that Shauntelle had sent him. He looked up, shot a quick glance back over his shoulder at her. All she could manage was a faint smile, then he turned away again, turned his horse to the left and headed along the edge of the clearing.

Once again he seemed to know where he was going. He looked up from time to time and then down at his phone.

And then her heart jumped as she heard the faint cries of her daughters. They grew louder as they moved along, and finally she could see her father in the open, watching them come.

The girls burst out of the greenery behind him and ran to Noah, calling out his name. And then they saw Shauntelle behind her, and for some inexplicable reason, they covered their faces with their hands and cried.

The universal reaction of a daughter in distress upon seeing her mother.

Shauntelle jumped off the horse so quickly she almost fell, and disregarding anything else, she ran straight to the girls, relief, joy and extreme gratitude flowing through her. She snatched them both into her arms, holding their little wet bodies close. They shivered with the cold. All she could do was thank the Lord that they were safe.

She kissed their wet cheeks and stroked their hair, and then pulled her coat off, trying to wrap it around both of them. Noah joined her, kneeling beside her daughters, pulling off his coat as well.

He slipped his over Millie and buttoned it up, then adjusted Shauntelle's coat over Margaret.

"You girls okay?" he asked. "Not hurt at all?"

"No. Just scared," Millie said. "Grandpa was keeping us safe, but he was scared too."

"We better get going before the girls get much colder," Noah said. He lifted Millie up into his arms. Then he turned to Shauntelle's father.

"How are you, sir?" he asked.

Her father looked rather shamefaced but also extremely relieved. "I'm fine."

Shauntelle didn't know which emotions to process first. She was angry with him for putting her daughters in jeopardy, and yet so relieved that everyone was okay.

Noah walked over to the horse and lifted Millie up

on his back, showing her how to hold the saddle horn. "Put Margaret on your horse," he said to Shauntelle, "and I'll lead them till we get to the creek." He glanced at her father. "I'd like you to ride with Millie. It will help keep her warm."

Her father nodded and, with Noah's help, got on the horse.

Then Noah started walking. To her surprise the ride back to the river seemed to take less time, and soon they were standing on the riverbank.

Noah turned to Shauntelle. "I'll ride with Millie, and you can follow me." Then to her father, "I'm sorry, sir, but I'll have to come back for you."

Again her father nodded.

Then Noah climbed aboard his horse behind Millie, slipped his arm around her and nudged the horse. It stepped into the raging creek.

Shauntelle was dismayed to see it was even higher than before. She had to fight down her own concern and trepidation as they made their way across.

The horses seemed to walk more slowly than they had on the way here. Of course, their load was heavier.

Noah let his horse have its head, and Shauntelle did the same. Her heart leaped into her throat when the horse set a foot wrong and slipped, stumbling and falling to one side. She imagined her and Margaret getting washed down the creek, but then it regained its footing and started again.

Finally the horses were on the opposite riverbank, and when they got to the other side, Noah lifted Millie off the horse, set her down and knelt beside her, tugging his coat closer around her. Shauntelle dismounted as well, guessing that her father would need to ride her horse. Without another word to her, Noah got on his horse, then walked across the creek again.

"Will Grandpa be okay?" Millie asked, her teeth chattering.

"He will."

"He will be with Noah, silly," Margaret said, shivering.

Shauntelle couldn't keep her eyes off Noah as he led the horse to the other side, then brought her father back.

When they were reunited, the girls hugged their grandfather and cried some more, and then Noah was lifting them onto the horses again.

"Why don't you get on behind Margaret again," Noah said to Shauntelle, then turned to her father. "And you should get on behind Millie.

"It's the best way to keep each other warm. I'll be walking so I'll be okay. We'll make better time that way."

Noah waited until everyone was mounted up, and then he took the reins of the horses and walked along the bank.

After a while the trees grew sparser, and they came to open fields and fences. They walked along the fences for a little while, turned a corner, and then, to Shauntelle's relief and gratitude, there stood the ranch buildings and the ranch house. Shauntelle had never been so happy to see a house in her life. They walked up to the corrals, and Noah tied up the horses as they all dismounted.

"You may as well all go into the house and dry up," he said to her and her father. He didn't meet their eyes, and Shauntelle didn't blame him. The whole time she was riding behind him, thankful for his presence, guilt blended with anger over what her father had done to him. She had wanted to apologize and explain, but now was not the time.

So she took her girls' icy hands and walked to the house.

Fay was standing on the deck, leaning on one crutch as they came to the house. "Come in, come in," she said, waving at them as if to hurry them up. "You must all be just freezing cold and hungry. I cannot imagine how difficult that must have been for you."

Shauntelle tossed a quick glance behind her and saw her father trudging some distance behind her, but still following them. The girls, clearly feeling quite at home, walked straight into the house.

Fay held the door open for Shauntelle and her father, and they both walked in. "You two must be absolutely freezing. I noticed you weren't wearing any jackets."

"No, we gave them to the girls," Shauntelle said, carefully removing her muddy boots and setting them aside. "But we rode behind them, so that helped."

She shivered again, then followed her daughters into the house, thankful for the blessed warmth.

Millie and Margaret were already by the fire, holding their hands out, still shivering.

"I'll make some hot chocolate," Fay said.

Then the door of the porch opened and closed, and Shauntelle sensed Noah was there. She couldn't stay. And she didn't think Noah would be comfortable with her father either.

"Thanks, Fay, but I think we should get the girls home as soon as possible," Shauntelle said, feeling ungracious. But she knew she couldn't be in the same room with Noah and her father. "Girls, we need to go."

"But surely you can stay—"

"We don't want to go," Millie cried out. "We're cold and we want hot chocolate."

"Millie. Manners," Shauntelle warned, hiding behind her Mom persona.

"Why do we have to go?" Margaret called out, not moving.

"We have to go home so Gramma won't worry about us."

"Just text her," Millie suggested, also staying right where she was.

Shauntelle felt torn between her father's discomfort and her own at seeing Noah again. It would be easier for all concerned if they left.

"Millie, Margaret, it's time to leave," Shauntelle said. "I need to bring Grandpa back to his car."

"I can take him."

Noah's quiet voice behind her sent her heart into a double-time rhythm. She took a few deep breaths to slow it down, and then a few more when the first did nothing.

"It's okay," her father said, looking down. "I don't want to be more of a bother than I've already been."

He looked ashamed, and he should. It had been his actions that had put her daughters in danger and, by extension, Noah and Shauntelle when they rescued them.

"Let Noah take him," the girls called out. "We're cold and wet." Millie added a dramatic shiver just in case Shauntelle didn't get the memo the first time.

"I don't mind," Noah said.

Shauntelle turned as he entered the kitchen. "You've done enough," she said, her voice quiet. She was unable to meet his gaze. "We can't thank you enough for helping us out."

"You helped too."

At that she looked up into his eyes and caught a glimpse of pain. But as quickly as it came, it seemed to disappear, his face growing impassive.

They had said little to each other on their rescue trip. There hadn't been a chance. But what could she say to him now?

I'm sorry my parents are suing you? I'm sorry that you thought I might have been a part of this?

"Anyway, we should leave," Shauntelle insisted.

"I would prefer to take your father," Noah said. His eyes never left her, but his voice held an edge and she guessed he wouldn't budge.

She glanced over at her father, who still stood where he was, eyes narrowed but looking down at the floor. Maybe it was for the best. Maybe it was time her father and Noah talked things out.

"Okay. I understand," she said, turning back to Noah. "Thanks for doing this," she said. "And thanks again for your help."

His only reply was a curt nod.

Then he turned and walked back to the porch, her father trailing along behind him.

Please, Lord, she prayed. *Please let my father be reasonable.*

It was all she could do now, she thought as she watched them leave.

Chapter Fifteen

As Noah started his truck, Mr. Rodriguez got in, looking as reluctant to come with him as the twins were to leave the ranch. He was sure Mr. Rodriguez's lawyer would advise him not to come along, but after what they had dealt with, taking a ride from him was more or less a moot point.

Noah backed out of the driveway, surprised at how nervous he felt. But it was Shauntelle he felt most concerned about. Did she agree with the lawsuit? Did she still think he was responsible for her brother's death?

Noah waited until they were on the pavement before he spoke.

"I know you might not believe me," he said, struggling to choose the right words. "But I want to say I am so sorry about Josiah. I'm sorry I didn't come to the funeral. I was told that because of the ongoing investigation, it was best I stay away. I want to tell you I should never have listened to that lawyer. I should have been there. And I apologize for seeming like I didn't care when, in fact, I did. Deeply."

The heavy silence that greeted his comment didn't bode well for the rest of the conversation.

Noah shivered, then turned the heat higher. He was still chilled and dealing with the aftermath of the pressure of rescuing the twins and Andy. He had been so thankful for the solid temperament of the horses they rode. When he saw how high the creek flowed, he had prayed harder than he had prayed in a long time. If anything had happened…

He stopped that thought. Nothing had. It all turned out okay.

"Please know not a day goes by that I don't think of your son and what I could have done better for him," Noah continued, hoping Andy would understand.

He knew Shauntelle loved her parents dearly and, as she had said many times, she owed them so much. He also knew how much she missed her brother. And because of her, he wanted to clear things up with her father.

"I think of him too," was all Mr. Rodriguez said.

They drove in an uncomfortable silence for a while, then finally Andy spoke up. "I want to thank you for coming to rescue me and the girls." He fidgeted a moment, then spoke up again. "This is hard for me to say, but I was irresponsible. I shouldn't have crossed the creek with the girls."

While Noah felt bad for Andy, given his obvious discomfort, he had to agree. Taking the girls across Horseman Creek, in the spring with rain in the forecast, had been irresponsible.

"I feel… I feel like a hypocrite," Andy continued, his voice small, quiet, as if the words were difficult to get out. "I said you were irresponsible and reckless with Josiah. But…I just did the same thing, and with my own granddaughters. I have no right to think I am better than you."

His admission astonished Noah. And beneath his words, Noah sensed a hesitant extension of an olive branch. If he and Shauntelle were to have any kind of future, and he hoped they could, he would have to find some way to resolve this issue in a way that would satisfy Andy.

"I don't know what your lawyer told you," Noah said finally, shivering as he warmed up. "I know we're not supposed to talk to each other, but I'd like to understand what you hope to get from this lawsuit. Is there some way I can help you without you going through all this expense and stress?"

Silence greeted that comment.

"What would you like from me?" he continued. "I've been sending you money. Do I need to send more?"

Andy sighed, then turned to him, but Noah only saw a hurt and broken man, not the angry one he expected. "I lost my son. Did you think money would replace him?" Andy asked.

"I never sent the money to replace him." Noah gripped the steering wheel even tighter. "I know I was absolved of all wrongdoing, but I kept thinking I should have done more for Josiah. I didn't send you the money because I felt it would replace him. I wanted to help you out."

"So you admit that you were guilty?"

Noah thought of what Shauntelle had said about Josiah's risk taking. He wasn't sure how to explain that to Andy without making it look like he was shifting the blame.

"I spent months trying to think of what I could've done differently," Noah admitted. "I've always prided myself on being a careful employer. But there's only so much I can do. There comes a point where an employee has to take responsibility."

And that's as close as he edged to suggesting that Josiah might have been at fault. He had no intention of talking ill about someone not present to defend himself.

"I really miss my son," was all Andy said.

"I believe you do," Noah said, the hurt in Andy's voice creating a surprising sense of melancholy. His father had always been so harsh with Noah. So unforgiving. Would he have grieved his loss the same way Andy was grieving Josiah's?

It wasn't a fair question, yet it clung.

"I also believe Josiah was a lucky young man to have people so concerned about him," Noah continued, remembering how Shauntelle had broken down in his arms, crying over losing her brother. "He was blessed to have people who loved him so much." He couldn't stop the small hitch in his voice. After all these years, he still hurt over how his father treated him?

"We loved him very much," Mr. Rodriguez said. "As I'm sure your father did you."

Noah released a harsh laugh. "I don't know how much my father cared for me. I know he was very hard on me, and that nothing I ever did was good enough."

"I'm sorry to hear that," Andy said. "That must have been difficult."

"I think he loved me in his own way. It was just hard to see."

"Maybe I could've been more careful with Josiah," Noah said, still hoping to find common ground between them. "But I did everything I could. You have to recognize that your son had to take some responsibility as well."

"I know." Mr. Rodriguez spoke so softly, Noah wondered if he'd heard right.

But the words created a spark of hope that they could come to some agreement.

Noah made the final turn, into the staging area where Mr. Rodriguez's car was parked. He pulled up beside it, but left his truck running. He turned to face Mr. Rodriguez, his arm over the steering wheel, his own emotions a mixture of thankfulness and uncertainty over what would happen.

"You need to know, I do not want to come between you and your daughter. I don't want her to choose between me and you."

Mr. Rodriguez nodded. "I understand that. And I respect you very much for that." He sighed again. "But I know that Shauntelle cares for you a lot. When I see how sad she's been the last few days, after you left, I know it's because she missed you. I don't like to see her unhappy. We've had enough sadness in our house." He paused again, his fingers tapping out a quick rhythm on his legs. "Selena and I were kind of pushed by our lawyer to sue and, I guess, by our own grief. It was easy to make you the bad guy and to think we could punish you. But I see how you are with our granddaughters, and I know they love you too. It hasn't been easy to change how we felt about you, but I see you are a good person. And I'm sorry I ever started this whole business. I thought this lawsuit would help us get over losing Josiah, but it only made us angrier and more stressed with each other."

Noah sat a moment, trying to sort out his thoughts. *Please give me wisdom*, he prayed. *Please give me the right words.*

"I'm not trying to tell you what to do," Noah said.

"I'm not a lawyer, but I think it would be a difficult battle after all the investigations proved neither I nor my employees were at fault."

Andy nodded, as if absorbing this information.

"You told me yourself that the money I sent you wouldn't bring your son back," Noah continued. "Even if— and it's a big if—you won this lawsuit, would that money make any difference?"

Then to his surprise, Andy Rodriguez covered his face with his hands and started crying. His sobs cut into Noah's heart, and he placed a comforting hand on his shoulder. He said nothing, just sat there hoping Andy felt his support.

Finally Andy stopped, wiped his eyes and gulped in a deep breath. "I am so ashamed. I accused you of being irresponsible, and then I go do this reckless thing with my granddaughters." He shook his head. "When I saw you coming through the clearing, my first reaction was relief, followed by a deep shame. My rescuer was the man I thought so little of. I couldn't face you, after all the things I had thought about you. And here you came to save my granddaughters. You truly are a selfless man."

"Anyone would've done the same," Noah said.

"I'm very thankful you did." Andy drew in a long slow breath, then looked over at Noah again. "I think I need to talk to my lawyer."

"You make the best decision for you and your family," Noah said. "I don't want you to think I had any influence on your choice."

"You don't need to worry. I had my doubts about the suit from day one. But that lawyer contacted us and kept calling and pushing. He said it was a way to take care of Shauntelle." He dragged his hand over his face.

"Josiah had always been the one who took most of our time and energy. He was always borrowing money from us. We never had enough to help Shauntelle out, and then she lost her husband and came to live with us and made plans for her restaurant. I thought, listening to our lawyer, that maybe we could finally help her too."

"I think Shauntelle is doing quite well on her own," Noah said. "She's a strong and determined woman."

"That she is." Andy slanted him a look full of regret. "Shauntelle was furious with us when she found out about the lawsuit. She said you didn't deserve to be treated this way. She told us that Josiah had always been reckless, and if we couldn't see that then we were blind. She was defensive of you. But she was also very sad when you left. She said she was making plans to move out. That hurt me and Selena a lot."

"And that's why I went to Vancouver. So she wouldn't have to choose between us."

"You were willing to make that sacrifice?"

"I know Shauntelle cared for me, and I care a great deal for her. More than I've ever cared for anyone before. But I also know she loves you and that you love her. I was sometimes jealous of your very intact family, and I didn't want to cause problems."

Andy held his gaze, looking as if he couldn't believe what he was hearing.

"Shauntelle has always been someone who knew her own mind. And someone who is wise and loving and kind. I was never that crazy about Roger. I had always thought she could do better. I would get so upset each time he put himself first, but she was a faithful wife and made that relationship work. Then I hear how you spend time with my granddaughters, how you went over and above to make sure Shauntelle got her doors installed in her restaurant. Without any hesitation, you came to help us. I also see how loving you are with your mother, and in all that I see a good person. In spite of what you may think of me and my wife, I realize maybe Shauntelle has finally found someone worthy of her."

His words fell like drops of mercy and grace into Noah's soul. He could hardly believe, after all the antagonism he'd been dealt by the Rodriguez family, her father was speaking like this.

"I don't know if I'm worthy of her," Noah said. "But I care a lot for her."

"Are you still moving to Vancouver?" Andy asked.

"I hope I have no reason to, if Shauntelle will still have me."

"Then maybe you better get back to the ranch and talk to my daughter before she leaves."

Relief and joy—and a curious peace—flowed through Noah. When he had said he would bring Andy back to his car, he had nurtured a faint hope of making peace. To show the man he cared about the loss of his son. That it mattered to him.

He had never dreamed it would turn out this way.

And then, as if to add another blessing to the day, the sun struggled through the breaking clouds.

"Come on, girls, now it's really time to go," Shauntelle said, glancing at her watch, struggling with a mixture of fear and trepidation.

Noah had been gone longer than it should have taken him to drive her father to his car. Were they arguing? Was her father spewing anger and frustration?

She had tried praying, but all she could manage was repeating *please, please* over and over again.

Mrs. Cosgrove seemed to sense her anxiety and,

Shauntelle was sure, suffered her own. After all, it was her son whom Shauntelle's father was suing. It was her son who stood to lose a great deal if this case went to court.

After Noah had left, Fay had served the girls their hot chocolate, set out a plate heaped with cookies, and then sat down in her easy chair by the fire. She made conversation with the girls, but after fifteen minutes Shauntelle could see she was getting tired.

Millie popped another cookie in her mouth, tilting her head as if thinking about her mother's comment. "I'm still a bit cold," she announced.

In any other situation, Shauntelle might have smiled at her daughter's machinations, but she was tense and on edge and wanted to get back home to talk to her parents. To see what had happened with her father and Noah.

And she could see that Mrs. Cosgrove felt the same.

"My pants are still damp," Margaret said, frowning as she rubbed her leg.

"I think your mother wants to leave," Mrs. Cosgrove said, sounding weary.

That did it.

"Girls. Now." Shauntelle put on her most firm voice.

Millie looked over at Margaret, and then, as if they both realized they had pushed the boundaries as far as they dared, they got up, walked over to Mrs. Cosgrove and each gave her a hug.

The sight sent a pang of desolation through her. What would happen now? How could they ever face Mrs. Cosgrove again?

Or Noah?

Shauntelle's heart seemed to fold at that thought.

What must Noah be thinking right now? Did she even want to know?

Chapter Sixteen

She was still here.

Noah breathed a sigh of relief, his hands releasing their death grip on the steering wheel as he pulled up beside Shauntelle's car.

He jumped out of the truck, slammed the door behind him and ran through the puddles to the house. Yanked open the door to the porch, stepped inside and almost ran into Shauntelle on the porch. She looked ready to leave.

Her eyes grew wide, and she pressed a hand to her chest, taking a step back.

"Noah's back," Millie cried out, running onto the porch to join them.

"Maybe we can stay longer?" Margaret put in.

Noah's eyes darted from the girls to Shauntelle, wondering what his next step should be. And then his mother appeared at the door. Her eyes held a question, and all Noah could give her was a small smile. He wanted to talk to Shauntelle before he said anything more to his mother.

"Actually, I'm feeling better," Fay said. "I think we should go into the family room to play a game."

The family room had a sliding door, separating it from the kitchen and dining room. It would give Shauntelle and Noah some privacy.

"If you don't mind staying a few more minutes?" Noah said, keeping his eyes on Shauntelle as if to gauge her reaction.

"Yippee! Let's go!" Millie cried out, never one to let an opportunity pass her by.

Shauntelle gave a slow nod as if considering her options. But the girls were already gone, his mother right behind them.

By the time he and Shauntelle entered the kitchen, the door to the family room was pulled shut and the girls' excited voices were muted.

They were alone.

"Do you want anything?" Noah asked, nervous, not sure where to start.

Shauntelle shook her head, her arms folded as if in self-defense.

Noah grabbed a quick drink of water, then turned back to her, his hands resting on the counter between them.

"So I spoke with your father," Noah said, his heart increasing its beat. So much rested on the next few things he said. "It was a good conversation, and I'm glad we had it."

Shauntelle's eyes grew wider, and she lowered her arms. "Did he talk about the lawsuit?"

"He explained how it happened, and that it wasn't only about Josiah. He and your mother hoped winning the lawsuit would let them help you. To make up for all the times they helped Josiah."

"Why did they think that?" Her voice held an edge of anger.

"They did it because they care about you. I think they felt guilty."

"The only thing they should feel guilty about is starting that lawsuit against you." Shauntelle held out her hands as if pleading with him. "Please know I had nothing to do with it. I had no idea you were sending them money."

She sounded so distressed, Noah couldn't stay where he was. He walked around the counter and pulled her into his arms.

"I had hoped you didn't." He stroked his hand over her head, relief, joy and peace he hadn't felt before flowing through him.

"And I should never have been as angry with you as I was." Her voice was muffled against his shirt.

Noah's only reply was to press a gentle kiss to the top of her head. "Anger is all part of the grieving process." And even as he spoke the words, he realized that his anger with his father might have been part of his own process.

She pulled back, a glint of tears in her eyes as she held his. "I'm sorry. I was wrong to think you had anything to do with Josiah's death."

"Nothing to be sorry about. You loved your brother, and you missed him."

Shauntelle released a hard laugh. "I did, but I was so angry with him when he died. I felt like he had done the same thing Roger had."

"And what was that?"

"Made promises he had no intention of keeping." She looked down, her fingers fiddling with a button on his shirt. "I think I took some of my anger with Roger and put that on Josiah, and then on you. You were a convenient target. I'm sorry. You didn't deserve that. You've been nothing but dependable, helpful and supportive."

Her words found a place in his own weary soul. "I don't feel like any of those things."

She gave him a gentle smile, then reached up and touched his face, her fingers tracing his jaw, rasping over the stubble and making him feel self-conscious. "You are. You sent my parents money even though you weren't at fault. You never, ever got angry with me, even though I wasn't always so good to you. You were the first person I thought of when I found out the girls were in trouble, and that told me a lot. I can depend on you."

"Except I took off."

A momentary hurt flitted over her face.

"I left because I didn't want you to have to choose between me and your parents," he explained. "Your family is close, and you guys feel each other's pain. In spite of what your parents did, I know they grieved Josiah's death, and that showed me how much they loved him. And you. I realize they sued because they love you. And, frankly, I am a little jealous of that love. Of that support."

Shauntelle's smile grew melancholy. "See? Again. You show yourself to be such a man of integrity, turning my parents' angry actions into something positive."

"I don't feel like such a man of integrity," he said. "I've done nothing heroic, like your husband did."

"What are you talking about? You crossed a raging river, drove through perilous underbrush, and rescued two damsels in distress and one irresponsible grandfather." Her smile softened, and she cupped his chin in her hand. "I would say that's heroic. I would say you're a man I would want to spend time with."

He cradled her face in his hands, studying her features, trying to think of how to say the words that were fighting to be spoken.

"I love you," Shauntelle said. "I love who you are, and everything you do. I don't care where we end up. I know you're a man I want at my side."

Now he could only stare at her, her words washing over him in a wave of love and grace. "How did I come to this? How did I get to this place and hear you say these beautiful things to me?"

"By being the amazing person you are," Shauntelle said, her voice trembling.

"I love you," Noah said. "And this may be rushing things, but I don't think either of us are in a place to dawdle. I think we both know what we want. At least, I know what I want. I don't have a ring, or a fancy proposal planned, or all the beautiful things you deserve. But I want to marry you. I want you in my life. You and those goofy girls of yours."

Her eyes shone and her lips trembled, then she nodded. "Yes. A thousand times yes."

He kissed her then, holding her close, still unable to believe this was all happening.

"They're kissing each other."

"Are they smiling?"

The whispering voices coming from the family room made Noah draw back. He kept his eyes on Shauntelle, unable to keep the smile from pulling at his lips. "I think we have company," he said to Shauntelle.

She closed her eyes, shaking her head. But with her arms still around Noah's waist, she turned back to the girls, who were peeking through the half-open door.

"You girls may as well come over here," she said, her voice light with laughter.

The girls needed no further encouragement. They tumbled out of the room and ran straight toward them.

"Are you guys getting married?" Millie asked point-blank.

"Nothing like cutting to the chase," Noah murmured. He caught Shauntelle's hand, then turned to the girls. "If it's okay with you, I would like to marry your mother."

"Can we live on the ranch?" Millie asked.

"Can we pick our own horses?" Margaret put in.

"Usually in a situation like this, we congratulate the people. We tell them how happy we are for them," his mother was saying as she approached the tableau.

Millie and Margaret exchanged hurried glances, seeming to contemplate what Noah's mother had said.

"Is it okay with you?" Noah asked again.

Margaret grabbed Shauntelle, and Millie threw her arms around Noah. Then to his surprise, they both started crying.

Noah shot Shauntelle a puzzled glance. "Does this mean it's okay?"

"I think it's been a long day," Shauntelle said, smiling.

She knelt and pulled both girls into her arms, holding them close.

"Are you happy about this?" she asked.

"So happy," Millie sobbed.

"I'm ecstatic," Margaret sniffed.

Shauntelle chuckled and then got to her feet. She rested her hand on Noah's shoulder and gave him a tender smile. "I think we're good."

Noah's mother joined them and gave Shauntelle a warm hug, then drew back. "I'm so happy for both of you. It's been a long, difficult journey, but I'm glad you both came home."

The girls rubbed at their eyes, then gave Noah and Shauntelle wide smiles.

"I guess this means we're going to be a family," Margaret said.

"It sure does," Noah said, bending over and picking her up.

"And I guess we could use a little brother," Millie said, sniffing. "I think brothers can be fun."

"Absolutely incorrigible," Mrs. Cosgrove said with a shake of her head. "At any rate, I think this calls for a celebration. I'm making hot chocolate and pulling out more cookies. We can all sit together and make plans."

The girls followed his mother to the kitchen. Noah turned to Shauntelle. "More plans? Are you okay with that?"

She smiled at him, then brushed a kiss over his cheek. "I love making plans."

"Plans for our family," he said.

"And a little brother?" she asked with a teasing smile.

"Let's take this one step at a time," he said.

"Someone has to take over when you're old and gray," she said.

He just laughed. She turned to join his mother and her daughters as they set mugs out and filled the plate with cookies. Their happy chatter filled the room that had long been devoid of joy and peace.

Thank You Lord, was all he could think. *Thank You for new chances and new hope.*

Epilogue

"Three years ago I would not have believed we would be here, together, in this amazing and finished facility," Cord Walsh said from his place on the podium, looking around the huge gathering in the finished arena. "It's been a long time coming, but thanks to us all pulling together, it happened. We have a place that will be used by the entire community, and we have an amazing restaurant that will also be appreciated by the entire community."

Cord gestured to Shauntelle, and everyone broke into polite applause.

"He's talking about you," Millie said, nudging her mother.

"I know, honey," Shauntelle whispered back. She looked over at Noah, who had Margaret perched on his shoulders, the two of them looking so at ease that anyone watching him would not have guessed she wasn't his biological daughter.

"There's many people to thank for this accomplishment. Noah for stepping in and helping us finish this, Reuben for giving us advice on how to do it and Morgan for his ongoing moral support. We also want to thank my father, Boyce Walsh, and George Walsh for their financial contributions. There's a plaque hanging on the wall in the foyer across from the restaurant that lists everyone who helped. Thanks for all you've done."

Owen Herne, who had been standing beside Cord all this time, applauded, then took over the mike.

"I can talk on and on about all the dreams and plans we have for the next rodeo, I can tell you about all the future events we'll host here, but you all know that already." Owen grasped the podium and looked around, smiling at his audience. "So I think we should get right to the celebration part of this thing. I declare this arena open for business. And I declare that we should eat the amazing food that Shauntelle Dexter—soon to be Cosgrove—prepared for us and that has been making my mouth water through Cord Walsh's long and boring speech. Let's eat and party and have fun!"

This was Shauntelle's signal to scurry over to the tables holding all the snacks she had worked so hard on.

"Can I give you a hand?" Leanne asked Shauntelle, appearing at her side.

"If you don't mind keeping an eye on the punch and the coffee, that would be great," Shauntelle said, tweaking a plate and adjusting a cloth as people lined up.

"I can make sure the plates stay filled," Tabitha offered.

"I don't know if you're the right person for the job," her fiancé, Morgan, teased her. "You and Nathan will probably spend more time eating than filling them."

Tabitha looked over at Morgan's son, who was already licking his lips. "Eating is good, right?"

He was rubbing his hands, eyes wide with anticipation. "Eating is perfect."

"Can we have a job?"

Shauntelle turned to look at Paul and Susie, Cord's children. "We can help, and we won't eat the cookies," Susie promised her, blinking her eyes much the same way Millie might have.

"I think you can help the twins," Shauntelle said, adding a smile. They hurried over to the table where the girls were helping Noah's mother hand out plates and napkins to the people lining up.

"You're looking a little frazzled," Noah said, joining her.

"Everybody wants to help, and I appreciate that, but I don't think I can supervise them all." She knew she shouldn't stress, but she so badly wanted everything to turn out well. She had spent days baking and all morning cooking.

"I wouldn't worry about that," Noah said, slipping his arm around her shoulder. "Check it out."

She looked in the direction he was pointing and saw her mother, Tabitha and Leanne Rennie, and Ella Walsh directing the kids, setting out napkins and hustling about, looking in charge.

"You're not on your own."

She drew in a deep breath, then leaned into his embrace, wrapping her own arms around his midsection, her ring flashing in the myriad of overhead lights in the arena. She looked around the space, new and still smelling of paint, and thought of her restaurant behind her, the doors open for people to sit inside and eat.

All around her people laughed and joked, ate and drank. She saw her parents chatting with Boyce Walsh, Cord's father. Her mother looked her way and smiled at her and Noah, as if granting her a small blessing. She and her mother had a long conversation after Noah and Shauntelle had gotten together. In it Shauntelle urged

her mother to let go of her anger and bitterness and forgive Noah. It had taken a few days but her mother had
slowly come around and now seemed happy for her.
Their eyes held a moment and then her mother's attention was caught by Millie and Margaret who were laughing at something Paul and Susie said. Ella had Oliver,
Cord's youngest son, perched on one hip as she deftly
served up savories. Ernest DeYoung, a horse trainer,
was deep in conversation with Morgan—probably vet-
related stuff.

Sepp Muraski, the owner of the Brand and Grill, was
inspecting the food laid out, sampling it and frowning.
Shauntelle had to fight a flicker of nerves. Sepp was
just being Sepp, she reminded herself. Kyle was talking to a group of people from the Farmer's Market who
were hanging on his every word.

"I still can't believe it's all come together," she murmured, resting her head on Noah's chest, filled with
such a rush of love for this man who'd helped make it
all possible.

"I can't either, but I can tell you one thing—I'll be
glad to hang up the hammer and be done with the responsibility of running a crew."

Shauntelle drew back to look up at him, giving him
an encouraging smile. "You did a fantastic job," she
said. "But then, you're such a fantastic person."

Noah smiled down at her and brushed a kiss over
her forehead. "I think you're biased."

"Not at all," she said. "I speak the truth." Then she
grew serious, tightening her arms around his waist.
"And the truth is, I love you and I love that we will be
a family."

"And you don't mind living on the ranch?"

"Why should I? That house is amazing."

"So you're just marrying me for my house?" he teased.

"Well, duh. I can't keep living with my parents forever."

He laughed, gave her another kiss, and then tucked a strand of hair behind her ear. "I love you, Shauntelle, and I'm so looking forward to living our lives together."

"Together. I like that word," Shauntelle said.

"Me too. And now, together, we're getting some food, and you're letting all these wonderful people take care of things."

She laughed, then nodded and followed him to where everyone was standing, laughing, eating and chatting.

Together.

* * * * *

If you loved this story, check out

COURTING THE COWBOY
SECOND CHANCE COWBOY
THE COWBOY'S FAMILY CHRISTMAS

from bestselling author Carolyne Aarsen's miniseries
COWBOYS OF CEDAR RIDGE

Available now from Love Inspired!
Find more great reads at www.LoveInspired.com

Dear Reader,

Grief hits us all in ways unique to each of us. A loss in the family is handled differently by each person.

In this book, Shauntelle was dealing with several varieties of grief. The loss of her husband, followed by the loss of her brother. On top of that, she was living with her parents, who were dealing with their own grief. When Noah comes to town, she has an easy target for the anger portion of grief that is often woven into sorrow.

Noah is struggling with his own guilt over the death of Shauntelle's brother, and seeing Shauntelle and her family's reaction to his presence in town only underscores that guilt. He didn't really want to come back to town, but obligation and the need to see his mother brought him there.

However, Noah has his own past and his own pain to deal with. His sorrow is connected to dark memories, hard work and a bad relationship with his father. He has to learn to separate past from present, which is the same lesson that Shauntelle and her family have to learn.

I hope you enjoyed reading the journey of Noah and Shauntelle as they learn to place their life in God's hands. As they learn to accept healing from the past. As they go forward into a new future together.

This is the last of the Cedar Ridge stories, and I hope you enjoyed your time here.

If you want to find out more about my books, check out my website at carolyneaarsen.com, plus you can write me any time at caarsen@xplornet.com. I love to hear from my readers!

Blessings,
Carolyne

LICNM0218

Get 2 Free Books,
Plus 2 Free Gifts—
just for trying the Reader Service!

YES! Please send me 2 FREE Love Inspired® Romance novels and my 2 FREE mystery gifts (gifts are worth about $10 retail). After receiving them, if I don't wish to receive any more books, I can return the shipping statement marked "cancel." If I don't cancel, I will receive 6 brand-new novels every month and be billed just $5.24 for the regular-print edition or $5.74 each for the larger-print edition in the U.S., or $5.74 each for the regular-print edition or $6.24 each for the larger-print edition in Canada. That's a saving of at least 13% off the cover price. It's quite a bargain! Shipping and handling is just 50¢ per book in the U.S. and 75¢ per book in Canada.* I understand that accepting the 2 free books and gifts places me under no obligation to buy anything. I can always return a shipment and cancel at any time. The free books and gifts are mine to keep no matter what I decide.

Please check one:

☐ Love Inspired Romance Regular-Print
(105/305 IDN GMWU)

☐ Love Inspired Romance Larger-Print
(122/322 IDN GMWU)

Name   (PLEASE PRINT)

Address   Apt. #

City   State/Province   Zip/Postal Code

Signature (if under 18, a parent or guardian must sign)

Mail to the **Reader Service:**
IN U.S.A.: P.O. Box 1341, Buffalo, NY 14240-8531
IN CANADA: P.O. Box 603, Fort Erie, Ontario L2A 5X3

Want to try two free books from another line?
Call 1-800-873-8635 today or visit www.ReaderService.com.

*Terms and prices subject to change without notice. Prices do not include applicable taxes. Sales tax applicable in N.Y. Canadian residents will be charged applicable taxes. Offer not valid in Quebec. This offer is limited to one order per household. Books received may not be as shown. Not valid for current subscribers to Love Inspired Romance books. All orders subject to approval. Credit or debit balances in a customer's account(s) may be offset by any other outstanding balance owed by or to the customer. Please allow 4 to 6 weeks for delivery. Offer available while quantities last.

Your Privacy—The Reader Service is committed to protecting your privacy. Our Privacy Policy is available online at www.ReaderService.com or upon request from the Reader Service.

We make a portion of our mailing list available to reputable third parties that offer products we believe may interest you. If you prefer that we not exchange your name with third parties, or if you wish to clarify or modify your communication preferences, please visit us at www.ReaderService.com/consumerschoice or write to us at Reader Service Preference Service, P.O. Box 9062, Buffalo, NY 14240-9062. Include your complete name and address.

LI17R3

Fresh off heartbreak, will Helen Zook find peace in Bowmans Corner...and love again with her new boss?

Read on for a sneak preview of
AN UNEXPECTED AMISH ROMANCE
by **Patricia Davids**,
available March 2018 from Love Inspired!

Mark Bowman lifted his straw hat off his face and sat up with a disgruntled sigh. Trying to sleep on a bus was hard enough, but the sound of muffled weeping coming from the seat behind him was making it impossible. He turned to look over his shoulder. The culprit was an Amish woman with her face buried in a large white handkerchief. She was alone.

"Frauline, are you all right?"

She glanced up and then turned her face to the window. "I'm fine."

It was dark outside. There was nothing to see except the occasional lights from the farms they passed. She dabbed her eyes and sniffled. She was a lovely woman. Her pale blond hair was tucked neatly beneath a gauzy, heart-shaped white *kapp*. He didn't recognize the style and wondered where she was from. "You don't sound fine."

"Maybe not yet, but I will be."

The defiance in her tone took him by surprise and reminded him of his six-year-old sister when she didn't get her way. Experience had taught him the best way to

LIEXP0218

stop his sister's tears was to distract her. "I don't care much for bus rides. Makes me queasy in the stomach. How about you?"

"It doesn't bother me."

"Where are you headed?"

"To visit family." The woman's clipped reply said she wasn't interested in talking about it. He should have let it go at that, but he didn't.

"Then someone in your family must be ill. Or perhaps you are on your way to a funeral."

She frowned at him. "Why do you say that?"

"It's a reasonable assumption. You'd hardly be crying if you were on your way to a wedding."

Tears welled up in her eyes and spilled down her cheeks. With a strangled cry, she scrambled out of her seat and moved to one at the rear of the bus, effectively ending their conversation.

Confused, he stared at her. Somehow he'd made things worse, and he had no idea what he'd said that upset her so. He shook his head in bewilderment.

Don't miss
AN UNEXPECTED AMISH ROMANCE
by Patricia Davids,
available March 2018 wherever
Love Inspired® books and ebooks are sold.

www.LoveInspired.com

Looking for inspiration in tales
of hope, faith and heartfelt romance?

Check out **Love Inspired®** and
Love Inspired® Suspense books!

New books available every month!